Chasing Nirvana

The sequel to A Contented Mind

By Samantha Hoffman

ISBN-10: 0-9848258-6-X
ISBN-13: 978-0-9848258-6-8

Dedicated to those who don't yet know they have wings.

And to my children, for giving me a reason to fly.

Excerpt from Wings To Fly

It wasn't that Madelyne hadn't tried. The truth that only she knew, was that she had spent her life - trying. Tired, she sat on the wooden porch swing behind her home. Unable to move, she didn't set the swing into motion. Instead she felt her mind, emotions and body shut down.

Since a small child, Madelyne felt set apart - alone, as if one foot was grounded in the world around her, while one foot remained elsewhere. To this day, elsewhere held promise, the world around her held isolation. Her only comfort was when what lived inside her spirit found its way onto a blank canvas. With every brushstroke, she watched the images form before her eyes like long lost friends taking shape and gathering for fellowship, laughter and comfort. Every painting brought with it peace of mind. Yet only moments ago, using thick, black strokes of oil, Madelyne brushed over and blackened not only the canvas in which her friends danced upon, but with every stroke she brushed over and blackened her soul.

Her husband's latest words, critical and accusatory in their intent, were the final shove that pushed Madelyne deep within herself. If one's heart is not allowed to live fully, expressing itself in its truest form, then it dies. The day Madelyne stopped painting, her spirit inhaled its last breath. It is a far greater loss when one loses their desire to live yet is forced to remain alive, then when one is given the chance to die as a whole.

Duty to her beautiful daughter required Madelyne to wake, to walk and to talk. What was left of her, was given for the purpose of raising Meg. It was through her daughter's eyes that she was able to glimpse the beauty of the world. And it was that beauty, seen through those eyes, that caused a natural smile to form across Madelyne's face whenever her daughter was near.

It had been months since her daughter asked the question that played like a skipped record inside Madelyne's mind. "Mom, how come you seem sad?" Like children do, her daughter asked what seemed like a simple question. But Madelyne knew the question only revealed that the demise of her soul had become evident. Evidence only noticeable to those who see with more than their eyes. A mother's pain rarely goes unseen by their child. Not only did Madelyne choose her words carefully when answering her daughter, while taking the long car ride to Buffalo, New York, but she had thought about it ever since.

People choose numerous paths when it comes to protecting oneself from pain. Madelyne chose to die inside; to isolate every part of her not required by her daughter. A death she felt would only be seen and felt by her and her alone. And in the process, she would no longer be open to the pain and disappointment inherent to life. Madelyne's hope was that somehow this internal death would release her from torment, and strengthen her efforts in raising Meg. But that one question proved her attempts had failed. Instead of liberating herself from pain, mourning privately within herself, she was forcing her daughter to live a life suspended in continual grief. The grief felt when watching a loved one die while still alive. A child hears what's being said without one word having been spoken.

No longer believing the venomous words of her husband; words that worked ardently to convince her that she would fail her daughter if she lived also for herself; Madelyne reached over and took her daughter's hand into her own; knowing that if her daughter had any chance of spreading her wings, she would first need to learn how to fly.

Madelyne held her daughter's hand as they walked out the door, eager to begin a life without the threat of watchful eyes. Filling her lungs with the fresh air of new possibilities, Madelyne looked down at her daughter and smiled. It was a smile that lit the world and the galaxies that lay far beyond.

"Time to fly," she whispered to her daughter, her eyes full of hope and promise.

Carefully crafting a life that held freedom firmly as its foundation, Madelyne stretched her large wings; spreading them across the world that now was hers. Living with the pain of the past, she stepped off the branch and let the energy that is life carry her across the clouds. She turned back only to smile, watching her daughter gracefully catch up with her. Together they swooped and danced as the brilliance of the sun swept across their beautiful wings. Content with what is, eager for what lies ahead.

That is the ending that should have belonged to my mother. Perhaps somewhere, in another lifetime, she is still flying beautifully, living the life that should have been hers. I will never know. I can only, when I am at my best, allow myself to dream that wishful dream.

Meg Kathryn Scott

Chapter 1

To Meg Scott, Fate was an enigma. Not the most polite or considerate of energies either. Never once did it stop to ask permission before entering her life. Fate, she felt, was similar to the negligent diner who fails to make reservations, yet walks to the front of the line, grabs whatever table it chooses then takes a seat. Fate never cares what Meg or anyone else thinks. But is Fate alone in its mischief, or is it the obedient, close-seated cousin of Providence, with its efforts admonished in the present, only to be praised once we look back.

"You sure this is where we're supposed to wait?" Chick asked, pacing the waiting room floor at Bay City Medical Center; the same floor he and his wife had paced only days ago.

"I'm positive, just sit down," Erin answered, tightening her arms across her chest.

"Where the hell is Jadon?" Chick looked around questioning, as if by sheer will he could see beyond the walls of the waiting room.

"He must still be talking with Dr. Solomon," Erin said. "God . . . I hope Meg's okay. I'm scared out of my mind." As Erin spoke, she scanned the serene art thoughtfully placed on the waiting room walls in an obvious attempt to soothe the anxious minds of its ever changing occupants.

"Christ, we don't even know what the hell happened," Chick reminded her, peering out the waiting room door. "Good. Here comes Stu and Bob. I just saw them walk off the elevator."

Walking into the neutral toned waiting room, Stu and Bob had the same look of scared confusion resting on their faces that was resting on Chick and Erin's.

"What the hell is going on? What happened?" Stu asked, rubbing his stubby fingers through his curly golden hair, his voice faltering under the weight of his worry. "God, Meggie better be all right. They said she was safe to be released yesterday morning, that her hemorrhage was safe enough for her to go home."

Bob searched Chick's face for a clue revealing why Meg had been rushed back to the hospital, then said, "She seemed fine when she left your house yesterday, Chick. Upset, but fine. What did Jadon say when he called?"

It had only been a day since the hospital had released Meg. But now Chick and the others found themselves standing in the same exact positions they were standing in a few days ago. With the same amount of crippling fear holding their bodies captive, everyone again waited, hoping Jadon would be able to make sense of the nightmare they were forced to relive.

"Why is Jadon going on the elevator?" Erin questioned.

"That can't be good," Chick mumbled.

Running down the hall, Chick tried to catch the elevator doors before they closed. Without breaking his stride, he rushed past the elevator, and ran down the stairwell. As Chick, pushed open the weighty stairway door, he saw Jadon walking out the entrance of the hospital. Hearing his name yelled behind him, Jadon turned, his face instantly showing his devastation.

"What the hell is going on? Jadon . . . Jadon!" Chick yelled, trying to snap Jadon out of his expressionless stare.

Jadon opened his mouth but no sound emerged. He couldn't give voice to the scattered words Dr. Solomon had just shared with him. Instead his mind was disabled by Meg's diagnosis.

"Jadon . . . Christ. What happened?"

"It's, uh . . . it's not good," Jadon said, pushing the words through the tears tightening his throat. "Um . . . Meg, uh, had a stroke. And, uh, they don't know yet, the level of damage. Oh, God. Chick . . . Jesus. Oh, my God."

"Oh, God . . ." Chick said, letting his body drop onto the sidewalk curb that bordered the front of the hospital. "How . . . what . . ."

"It's my fault. I did this to her, Chick. I mean . . . the doctor was so serious when he told me . . ."

"Jadon, this isn't your fault. None of this is your fault. Dude . . . things happen. After you left my place yesterday, what happened? The doctor said for her to take it easy. I mean, what happened?" Chick asked, squinting into the hazy California sunlight to look up at Jadon. "Sit down. Tell me what happened."

Slowly sitting down, Jadon rested his arms on his knees and stared at the parking lot sitting across from them, not knowing where to begin, or how to explain the events that led to Meg's stroke.

"Uh, well, we left your place. I took Meg home, you know. And she stood on the balcony for a while." Jadon paused. "She missed seeing the ocean. She loves to just quietly stare at the water."

"Good. That sounds fine."

"Then, well . . . I thought she was tired. And she was," he said, turning to look Chick in the eye. "So I put her on her bed, and . . ." Jadon stopped, looking back at the cars moving slowly through the parking lot.

"Did she go to sleep?"

"No." Not breaking his stare across the street, Jadon shook his head.

"Was she real upset about Bobby? I know that was hard on her. I mean I know he was a dog, but he was more human than almost anyone I've ever known. He was also her best friend, until you. And the way he died. With you guys trying to rescue him from the river, then she thought you were going to die, then she . . . she's the one that almost dies. I mean . . . Christ, that had to be ricocheting through her mind," Chick said, turning to watch a small group of visitors with balloons that danced in the breeze make their way through the entrance of the hospital.

"She was upset. But she seemed almost peaceful about it. I think it was that dream she had. Where she saw her mom walking with Bobby and Stinky. I think that helped her put his death in a better place."

"Did she fall down?"

"No, no. God, Chick, we did the one thing, the one thing Dr. Solomon was adamant about us not doing."

"You didn't . . ."

"Yeah, yeah. Christ! I couldn't stop myself. And now God only knows what's going to happen."

Staring across the street, both Jadon and Chick sat speechless. Chick grabbed a cigarette from his pocket, nervously lit it and handed it to Jadon before lighting another for himself.

"That couldn't have been . . . what caused this Jadon . . ." Chick said compassionately.

"Well . . . pretty fuckin' coincidental then. Christ. The doctor sits me down and says for us to absolutely not make love. We make love. Here we are. And now, we don't know if she's even going to make it. And if she does . . . if the clot damaged anything . . . God!" Jadon wiped the tears from under his pale blue eyes. "I got her here within minutes. I mean . . . I fuckin' flipped out. We were standing on the balcony this morning, and I just handed her a cup of coffee. And she was so content. And . . ." Jadon paused while a shiver of fear worked through his body. "Then smash. The cup falls, and down she went."

Putting his arm around him, Chick tried to comfort his closest friend while he cried silently. Jadon's body trembled softly from the uncertainty of Meg's condition and also from the weeks and months that led to this moment. It had been only two weeks since the band went on their camping trip in the mountains near the Kern River after finishing the European acoustic rock tour. And only a few days had passed since Meg had been rushed into the Southern

California Neurological Center. Fate, in cruel irony, had allowed Meg to suffer a brain hemorrhage when her beloved dog Bobby kicked her with his hind leg as she tried rescuing him from the Kern River. The image of Meg's body floating next to Bobby while he struggled to set himself free from a thick web of fallen branches that had his paws entangled still rested in the forefront of Jadon's mind.

"Is she responsive? I mean, are her eyes open?" Chick asked.

Sitting up straighter, Jadon tried to rein in the thoughts racing through his mind. He snubbed out his cigarette on the curb, shuffled his feet, then glanced back at Chick.

"No, no. Did you know there's a 40 percent mortality rate with this type of stroke? Isn't that fuckin' great? Oh, God," Jadon said, choking back another lunging cry.

"Well, then, that means there's a 60 percent survival rate, right?" Chick said, trying to make eye contact with Jadon.

Feeling a morsel of comfort from Chick's words, Jadon glanced over at him, "Yeah. I mean, yeah, I guess so."

"Okay, let's start there. Our Meg is like a superhero. She's going to beat this. I know it. It won't be long and Equinox will be back in the studio making kick ass rock music again, gearing up for more shows. And you two will be doing that thing you were doing on your balconies," Chick said, fluttering his hand in the air, not sure how to describe the romantic interludes Jadon and Meg had been sharing for months before ever knowing who the other was.

Jadon let out a soft chuckle. "Yeah, yeah. She's strong. I tried not to . . . I told her no. I mean, I thought I was going to literally die saying no. But I did . . . "

Chick kept his eyes focused across the street. He knew Jadon needed to explain, and hopefully in the process release some of the crushing guilt sitting on his shoulders. Chick was certain the guilt was unfounded, but he didn't blame him for having it, either. Jadon's love for Meg was more than what most people felt when they easily whispered those three simple words: *I love you*. Between Jadon and Meg, those words transcended what many could even handle. It had been that way from the moment they first saw one another when Meg showed up for an audition to join the band. When their eyes fell in line with one another, time stopped. And everyone standing around them knew something of cosmic proportions was taking place, even if at first it was hard to decipher what the energy swirling around the two was. But there was never any denying that the energy was there. And as time went by and Fate's mischievous and sometimes life-threatening obstacles had been overcome, it was easy to see theirs was a destined love. It was the kind of love that Fate — or perhaps Providence — purposefully makes certain happens by moving people, circumstances and situations. Once Meg and Jadon were brought together, it felt like the world would stop spinning if ever they separated. As Jadon and Chick sat outside the hospital, it was obvious to both that if the earth were to stop spinning, now was the time.

"I wanted to make love to her more than I wanted to live another day, ya know?" Jadon said, slowly sharing what was resting heavily on his mind. "She asked me to lie down next to her. I did. And I told her if anything ever happened to her . . ."

"It's all right. Let it out. It's all right. She's gonna' be all right. And this isn't your fault. This probably would've happened anyway," Chick said, trying to calm Jadon's reeling mind.

Shaking his head, Jadon said, "No. I don't fuckin' believe in coincidences. God, sometimes I wish I did. Ya know? I mean if I just thought shit happened, things would seem so much easier. But I know, he said not to. We did. And now I don't know if I'm going to be able to fly with her."

"Where you guys going?"

"No, not that kind of flying. I, uh . . . right before we fell asleep in each other's arms. I asked her how to ask a woman who doesn't want to ever marry, but I want to spend the rest of my life with . . . how to ask her to be with me forever.

And she looked so beautiful lying there, her long red hair draped over her shoulder." Jadon paused, not realizing how painful the vision of Meg would be. "She thought about it a minute. And she turned to me and said, *just ask . . . would you fly with me?*"

"Oh, that sounds like what Meg would say, all right. So . . . what'd you say?"

"I asked her to fly with me," Jadon said, raking his fingers through his long blonde hair.

"I *think* I know the answer she gave," Chick responded.

Keeping his eyes held on the parking lot in front of him, Jadon smiled. "She looked at me with those big hazel eyes of hers and said, *As long as I'm blessed to do so, there's no place I would rather be than flying next to you.*"

Turning to look at Chick, Jadon couldn't hold back his tears. Chick again put his arm around his friend and held him tight. Looking around, Chick questioned how life could be so unkind. Over the past few months he watched one cruel event play out after another. All of which made him wonder how Fate worked, or if Fate was even a friendly concept. All of his life he thought it was something leading to one's own nirvana. Now, sitting next to Jadon with the warm sun beating down on them, he had to wonder if there was a God. And if so, did she control Fate or was everyone just a sitting duck, waiting for life to pull the trigger and take another deadly shot?

"I can't lose her, Chick. I finally, finally . . . after all this time, after all the hurdles, got her. How can life be so messed up?"

"I don't have a fuckin' clue, man. I'm dumbfounded. God. I thought things were finally going to be smooth sailing. Devon's gone, or at least out of the picture. Sure, Bob is gone, but . . . he was a good dog, ya know. And I think he did what he was meant to do. He kept Meg company till you two could be brought together."

Listening to Chick's words, Jadon threw his face into his hands. Unable to speak, he listened as Chick tried to make sense of life and the tumultuous turn it had once again taken. He remembered the afternoon last fall when Meg walked into the band's studio with her violin, and the way she overwhelmed them with her passionate, soulful playing. As the weeks passed, Jadon had learned that her virtuoso passion and intensity reflected a long and painful struggle to heal her heart after her parents' death when she was just a young girl. It was that same pain that also caused her, enabled her, propelled her to write best-selling novels, and yet caused her to do so using a pseudonym, keeping her life hidden behind a thick curtain she purposely pulled closed.

Some families are formed from birth, others by Fate. In the latter category was Equinox, the family Meg longed to discover. Because of her sensitivity and quick wit, she easily and quickly won the hearts of the band members, who loved her like a sister. All except for Jadon, who fell head over heels for her, not just when he met her at the studio but when he first heard her play her violin standing alone on her balcony next to his house.

⚘

With his arms folded across his chest in relaxed ease, Devon Mitchell Hathaway leaned his tall, distinguished frame against the window ledge in his penthouse at the Hathaway Hotel in the Westminster borough of London. Far below was the Thames River and in the near distance sat Westminster Abbey. Devon had the natural ease of one who inherited a great deal of money and made a great deal more in the hotel and publishing businesses. In the center of Devon's mind were the words his assistant had just shared with him; now his thoughts were far away, in Southern California. The one thing Devon felt sure of was that, once back in the States, he would not leave until he knew Meg was going to recover. And once she did, he still wasn't going anywhere until she turned her love back toward him.

Combing his fingers through his dark hair, Devon tried to relax the muscles on his face; muscles held tight from the damage he had done. He hadn't underestimated Meg's love for Jadon; he knew it was there, and he hated that it was there. He had, however, believed he could overpower it. It was among the few miscalculations he had ever made in his forty years of life.

Turning slowly, Devon walked toward the fireplace. As he stood in front of the fire, he stared at the soft amber flames, and contemplated the timing of Meg's stroke. Within months the book she wrote under her own name, published not by his publishing company but another, would be released, and that meant soon her new publishing company would demand that she promote it. Meg had never endured the rigors of a book tour, with signings at book stores, talk show appearances, and interviews with their always repetitive and often inane questions. Her nom de plume and passion for secrecy had spared her all that. Devon knew that now more than ever Meg would need a strong, guiding hand to help navigate the waters she had never before sailed. Picking up his phone, Devon smiled, knowing that on these choppy waters Jadon wouldn't be the one holding the life raft.

"I know, Trish . . . this will be quite a trying time for Meg. I know," Devon said, trying to lighten his strong

British accent, after listening intently to Meg's new publisher at Handle House Publishing express her concerns. "I will do all I can," he paused, paying careful attention to every word Trish shared with him on the other end of the phone. "I think it best, however, to let Meg move forward with this on her own if possible. I will do all I can, but let's not mention that we spoke. I don't want Meg to feel I have in any way . . . stepped on her toes. I wouldn't want her to feel slighted. I'm sure you understand. Let's keep in touch, and together . . . we will make sure Meg promotes this book exactly as she is contracted to do so. Keeping in mind, of course, her current condition. Very well, as always, it's been wonderful speaking with you again."

Flipping his phone closed, Devon looked over his calendar and cleared all of his appointments that interfered with Meg's upcoming media engagements. To strategize well, one has to be willing to make sudden changes, and if Devon was anything, he was willing to shape-shift into whatever form needed to accomplish his desires.

Chapter 2

Flora walked into the hospital waiting room. Searching for Erin, she slowly scanned the scattered faces; finding her seated with her face nested within her hands. Flora walked slowly in her direction and stood before her. Her long dark curls, accented by silvery gray, shrouded her face as she looked down.

"I'm here," Flora said calmly.

Hearing Flora's low, steady voice, Erin was immediately comforted. She wrapped her arms around Flora and held tight. Flora smiled gently; it was a smile created by the image forming in her mind as soon as she touched Erin.

"Erin . . . do you feel all right?"

"No. Nothing about me feels all right. I feel horrible. God, no one will tell us what's going on with Meg. We just know she collapsed. Chick is outside with Jadon. But Jadon didn't even stop to talk to us. He just left. It's not good,

Flora, is it?" Erin asked, her fear easily seen once she pulled her long brown hair behind her ears.

"I need to go and see her, Erin. I don't like what I'm feeling about this. I want to sit with her, and then I'll know more. I'm too connected to separate my fears from what I *know*," Flora said slowly.

"They're not letting anyone in. I don't even know if Jadon is allowed in. God, Flora, he didn't look good when he got on the elevator."

"I know. I saw him as I walked in. I didn't stop. It wasn't the time. Chick was holding him. He's hurting. He feels guilty."

"Why would Jadon feel guilty?"

"He shouldn't. This would have happened regardless. I'm angry, Erin. And I don't like that I'm so angry. I'm not centered right now. I don't like that this happened *when* it did. It makes me question the beauty of this world," Flora said, breaking her eyes from Erin to look out the window.

What Flora revealed through her words and the expression on her face made Erin worry all the more. To Erin, Flora was like a magical creature, that stood perfectly balanced so she could easily move between the earthly world and the spiritual world; the one held invisible to most. But within the current moment, it was evident Flora couldn't help herself from stepping off the balanced platform she normally stood upon.

Possessing more wisdom than the half century she had lived could ever provide, Flora had always viewed life through a vast, open window. Regardless of the circumstances, she saw multiple layers. Her gentle spirit had the ability to rule her mind, and thus allow her to hear the secrets those many layers whispered. The beauty of the Universe was often buried deep within a labyrinth of situations that to most made the Universe appear chaotic and cold. But ever since Flora was a small child, she saw that which sat behind the chaos, and therefore saw the beauty in all things — except for today. Today she saw only cruelty. And the many layers that might reveal hope and answers were closed to her.

"Jesus, Flo . . . you're scaring the shit outta us with that look on your face," Stu said, looking over at Flora, then up at Bob, whose gaze was also held steady on Flora.

"I'm sorry. I just don't feel anything but anger. I can't see anything but my anger. I need to be alone with God before I'm alone with Meg," Flora said, gracefully walking out of the waiting room and away from the anxious eyes that hoped she would have the answers no one else had.

☙

Sitting on a large warm rock, Meg slowly surveyed the open field surrounding her. The goldenrod and violet wildflowers that carpeted the ground brought a calming smile to her face. She took her time absorbing the presence of each one as she tried to ignore the overwhelming awareness of where she was. She knew this place, and this place knew her. It was not like the typical countryside that normally sat beyond a row of houses; instead, this place was held apart from the world she normally walked through. But it was warm, and she could feel the sun soak through her body, even though she knew if she looked up, she wouldn't find the sun sitting in its normal place above her.

To her left Meg saw a large hawk swoop down and glide over the wildflowers. With her eyes still captivated by the gold and amber weeds that delicately revealed the shape of a small hill, Meg watched as the same tall weeds parted abruptly.

"Bobby?" Meg questioned.

Running at full speed, a speed she hadn't seen her Irish setter travel since he was a pup, Bob rushed into Meg's open arms. Falling gently off the rock, Meg landed on the soft ground with her arms wrapped around Bob's wavy auburn fur. She ran her hands over his gentle face and looked tearfully into the only eyes that had ever understood her.

Bob rubbed his head into hers, then let out a soft bark. Wagging his tail he quickly sat next to Meg as they both watched Madelyne walk through the field toward them. Wiping the tears from her face, Meg kept her arm wrapped around Bob while she kept her eyes held softly on her mother. Madelyne sat down on the rock next to Meg, turned to look down at her, and smiled. Meg gazed at her mother's face. The last time she saw her mother she hadn't been allowed to be so close to her. Meg wanted to be close to her, now more than ever, but in being allowed to do so, she feared what it meant.

"Am I . . . dead?" Meg slowly whispered.

"No," Madelyne said softly, tilting her head compassionately toward her daughter.

"Well . . . you're here. And I'm here. This . . . this can't be real good. Even though it feels good," Meg cried. "I mean, Bob's here. And . . ."

"Sweetness," Madelyne said softly, brushing her hand across Meg's cheek, "don't be upset. Sometimes it's almost impossible to understand what is unfolding, and why. The ways of the Universe . . . well, let's just say sometimes they are opposite of how our human mind works."

"Well, you've got that right," Meg said, looking into her mother's luminous eyes. "You can't even be here. And yet here you are. And here I am. God, I'm not quite ready to . . . "

"I need you to *trust*, my dear. Just trust," Madelyne said calmly.

"Trust what? God? Does God hate me? Is that it? Because that's the only thing that even comes close to making sense. I just found my place in this world."

"You've always had your place."

"Well, then, how come I'm not in it at the moment? This place we're in now . . . it's not . . . normal. Am I dying? I don't want to die, Mom. I want to live."

Madelyne looked over the hillside. Gently placing her hand over her daughter's, she gazed out at the far reaching skyline and took her time before saying anything. She knew she had to choose her words carefully. She was called because she was needed. But it was a delicate line separating what information would help her daughter, and what would hurt.

"This journey that you're on, Meg, it is for *you* to travel. You aren't done yet, my dear. Not yet."

Staring at her mother, Meg couldn't find a great deal of comfort in what she was hearing.

"I know you want clear answers, sweetness," her mother continued, while keeping her eyes held steady on the horizon in front of her. " Please know, there aren't any. There is only that which you believe. And your journey is to fulfill a higher purpose. There is a reason, sweetness. There is a reason for everything."

"Well, I really don't understand, Mom. I . . . I'm trying, but . . . is this what karma is? Was I a horrible person in a past life? I was Attila the Hun, wasn't I? Oh, God, not Hitler. Was I Hitler, and now I'm paying for it? I've never understood the concept of karma as I always thought it was wrong to make one person pay for something they didn't even know they did, but . . ."

"No, dear. No, you have done nothing wrong." Madelyne smiled.

"Am I supposed to ignore then the wicked cycle of events that have occurred in my life? Am I supposed to just act like horrible things don't happen?"

"It's what you do with those events, dear. It's what you do with them that matters. Sometimes it is the only way the Universe can get our attention."

Meg stared at her mother, dumbfounded by her words.

"What about Jadon?" Meg's voice cracked softly. "What is he? I love him, Mom, I love him."

"The Universe answered your call. You asked for him. And he asked for you."

"I don't remember asking . . ."

"You asked, but not with words. Nor did he," Madelyne smiled again. "Sweetness , I have to go. What you need to do is trust. There is no good or bad in the eyes of the Universe. Remember that. Remember to trust in what you believe. And, my dear girl, believe in what you *want*. Then stand firm and trust."

Madelyne leaned over, placed her lips on Meg's forehead, and gave her a maternal kiss. Looking into Meg's eyes, she smiled.

Meg watched as her mother and Bob slowly made their way back through the field, and beyond the small hill, until they slowly vanished over ridge line. Throwing her face into her hands, Meg sobbed. She realized she felt no more clarity or understanding than she had before. Looking through watery eyes at the hilltop over which her mother and Bob disappeared, Meg felt nothing but anger.

Shaking her head, Meg shouted, "Goddamn you! Goddamn you! You . . . whoever you are. You're like a beautiful thief that walks in and out of my life taking away the most important things. You want me? Is that it? What's in store for me now, huh? Goddamn you! Why can't you be my friend? Why can't you talk to me? Is it that I'm not learning, is that it? Is that why you put me through hell. I just want to live my dreams. Is that too much to ask?"

~

"Mr. Hastings. Good, you're here. That was quick," the nurse said with a smile, noticing it had only been minutes since she left a message on Jadon's cell phone. "Dr. Solomon would like to speak with you. You can go inside now. You can join him too Mr. Holschick."

Stepping into Meg's room, Jadon felt the familiar swift plunge of his heart as he looked at Meg lying helpless in the hospital bed. The only sounds in the room were the hums and clicks of the monitors, reminding everyone that, despite appearances, Meg was still alive.

"Jadon, why don't you sit down?" Dr. Solomon suggested gently, motioning to the chair next to Meg's bed.

With their movements echoing the numbness that blanketed their bodies, both Chick and Jadon sat down, not taking their eyes off of Dr. Solomon as he walked slowly over to other side of Meg's bed.

"Meg hasn't come to, yet," Dr. Solomon began. "There has been damage to the brain. Until she wakes, we won't know the full extent. But the scans do show significant signs of . . . of damage."

"When will she . . . ?" Jadon stammered.

"Wake up? We aren't sure. We also aren't sure how to interpret the intense amount of brain activity she's experiencing," Dr. Solomon said, glancing down at his notes.

"What does that mean?" Chick said quickly. "I mean . . . it feels like we don't know anything here."

"I understand how upsetting this is, Mr. Holschick. Please know that medical tests and scans give us a great deal of information. But each person is different. Everyone reacts slightly different, everyone heals slightly different."

"What do you mean . . . brain activity?" Jadon asked.

"Well, to put it simply, it's almost as if she's awake. We haven't sedated Meg. She is unconscious due to the trauma. And yet, her mind is very much awake, so to speak. We aren't confident how to interpret it," Dr. Solomon said, shaking his head.

"Why the hell can't we have clear answers? It's like we don't fuckin' know anything, ever," Chick said, his voice matching the rapid beats of his heart.

"Well . . . this could be good, right?" Jadon asked, looking at Chick, then back at Dr. Solomon.

"I think so. I think so," Dr. Solomon answered.

"Think?" Chick said hastily.

"Mr. Holschick, as I said, I understand how upsetting the uncertainty of this is. I believe it is important for you to know our findings, even if I can't give you a clear answer as to why something is happening." Dr. Solomon explained, his words falling steadily into place as he calmly said them.

"I know. Thank you. Thank you. I'm just . . . I just feel like we're all floating around here not knowing shit about shit."

"Medicine isn't an exact science," Dr. Solomon replied with a compassionate smile. "We do more floating than we want. But . . . the best we can do is learn how to keep the sails up and the boat running. You can stay with her until she is taken to the third floor. They should be getting her room ready. It should only be a few more minutes."

Chick and Jadon sat quietly as they listened to the heavy door softly sweep across the floor before it shut behind them. Getting up slowly, Jadon stood next to Meg. He looked down at her face, wiped the tears from his own, then bent down to kiss her head gently. Sliding next to Meg, Jadon rested his head next to hers.

"God, I don't know anymore what the fuck is going on," Chick said, walking over to Jadon. "I'll be out in the waiting room. I need to tell Erin. She's pretty anxious. You . . . you tell Meg we all love her."

Nodding his head, Jadon tried to ignore his fears. He smiled softly as he gently ran his finger across Meg's eyebrow and down her cheek before touching her lips. Kissing her softly, Jadon kept his head rested onto hers.

"So here we are again. And I'm scared to death again," Jadon whispered, deciding not to give life to the fears wanting to be born inside his mind. "I don't know what to think. But I know you couldn't have been brought clear across the country, bought a home next to mine, and been the perfect match to my heart . . . if we weren't meant to fly together. That I know."

≈

Before Chick had a chance to enter the waiting room, Stu darted around the doorway. Running his hands through his long black hair, Chick felt his throat tighten from both fear and anger. Looking back at Stu, Chick shoved his hands into the pockets of his faded black jeans.

"It's fucked. That's what this is," Chick said.

"What . . . what does that mean?" Stu asked, glancing at everyone as they gathered behind him.

"This whole thing. All of it. It's just wrong," Chick struggled to say, realizing the only thing he was revealing was his frustration.

"Babe, we don't know what you're trying to say," Erin said softly, stepping in closer. The look on her husband's face showed he was crumbling under the weight of Meg's prognosis.

"Uh . . . Meg had a stroke. She's unconscious. Although she has a great deal of brain activity, they don't know what the hell it means. Could mean anything. There's a forty percent chance she might not make it. Sixty percent chance she might pull through. They really don't know anything until she wakes up. The doctor did say the tests show there has been considerable damage from the stroke." Chick paused. "It's not right. This, this whole thing."

"What happened. How did this happen?" Stu asked.

"It just happened. Jay said she collapsed this morning. He rushed her right here."

"How is Jadon?" Bob asked.

"Not good. He's with her now. It's as if we're right back where we were a couple days ago. He . . . loves her so much." Chick's words cracked, then ended.

Erin, Chick, Bob and Stu watched as Flora walked off the elevator and down the hall toward Meg's room. Without saying a word, they knew Flora was being drawn toward Meg.

Jadon opened his eyes at the sound of the door and watched Flora walk to the side of the bed. Putting her hand first on Meg's head, Flora then slowly and purposefully let her hand glide softly over Meg's body, stopping to put Meg's hand in her own.

Looking at Jadon, Flora said quietly, "Don't blame yourself. And don't blame your love." She closed her eyes and paused before continuing. "Your love has kept her alive and fighting."

"But Flora . . . ," Jadon tried to explain.

"No. This would have happened. I know that. I don't know how or when. But it would have. This, as cruel as it appears, happened for a reason. I'm not able to see why right now. I'm closed off more than normal. I don't have the layers of clarity I know so well. I only see your pain, and my anger. But I do see the essence of this . . . and it was going to happen, one way or another. And so it has."

"Why are you closed off? What does that mean?" Jadon questioned, keeping his head rested on Meg's.

Letting out a soft chuckle, Flora answered, "I'm very angry right now. But it's the truth of how I feel, and I need to give this feeling the time it needs. A denied feeling only grows."

Flora felt Jadon's eyes held steadily onto her own; eyes that questioned what she meant. "I'm angry about the timing of this. You two were brought together by Fate, but Fate chose *now* to do *this*. Malevolent timing."

Leaning over Meg's bed, Flora slid her hand over Jadon's face. Like a mother, hoping her caress would ease the fears of their child, Flora hoped something in her touch would ease the nightmare in which Jadon was living.

"There is a lot I don't know. But I do know there is magic between you and Meg," Flora said gently, stopping for a moment to look carefully into Jadon's eyes before walking out the door.

Sliding closer to Meg, Jadon thought about Flora's words. He wanted instead to think about the beautiful moment he shared with Meg the night before. Their lovemaking and the words she shared with him after. But all he could see was Meg collapsing onto the balcony, and knowing that he had caused it.

Jadon's cell phone vibrated lightly in his pocket. Sliding out the phone, he read the name illuminated by the soft blue backlight, and let out a faint, deflated sigh. The same simple sigh that accompanied every form of communication he had with his father. Jadon hit the ignore button on his phone, and slid it back into his pocket. There was a No Vacancy sign in his mind and in his heart when it came to his father. Not that he would ever illuminate that sign for his father to see. Instead, it was a reality Jadon kept only to himself, until Meg.

"Looks like Dad's calling, Meg," Jadon whispered, burying his head into Meg's neck. "Sooner or later you'll be meeting the illustrious John Hastings. Not that it's anything to worry about. He's fine. On the outside, anyway."

⁓

Reclined in the deep blue chaise lounge chair behind his house, overlooking the ocean, Chick blinked slowly, and wondered if the sun he was watching set before his eyes was trying to tell him something. Never being naturally inclined to decipher hidden meanings, least of all those given by nature, Chick couldn't ignore the unsettling vibrancy of the sunset, and wondered what it meant.

Taking its time before nestling behind the vast Pacific Ocean that waited patiently its arrival, the sun expressed itself in the only way it knew how, through color. A scene that gave Chick reason to pause, noticing every brilliant shade of delicate pink that blended perfectly with the floating lines of purple that swept casually across its surface.

"Okay . . . so what's this mean? You've been kickin' us around a lot lately. What are ya trying to say?" Chick asked, taking a cigarette out of its pack. "Lay it on me, Big Guy. I'm all ears."

His raw sarcasm didn't soften the stirring emotions he felt inside as he watched the sun appear to stop its descent. Instead he felt his body tremble. After a momentary pause, the sun continued to blend into its surrounding colors, creating a fiery burst of color that if painted, would've caused its admirers to conclude it was done so by the hand of an amateur — one not knowing how to modestly use color to show nature in its truest form. As if God were that novice painter, proud of his steady brushstrokes, the sun carried with it a darkened line revealing its perfectly rounded shape. Not wanting to blink, Chick continued to stare, knowing only that he was supposed to be aware of what he was watching. Slightly exposed, the sun then surrendered to the embrace of the ocean, and in doing so softened into a wave of red and orange before wrapping itself completely behind the blue blanket of the Pacific.

"Hey," Erin offered lightly, taking the cushioned lounge chair next to Chick's. "Missed the sunset. I actually tried to get out here, too," she chuckled, letting her exhausted eyes linger on the glow that still remained seated over the ocean. "You're too quiet, babe."

"Yeah, I know," he answered, giving her a warm grin before turning to look back at the water. "I know."

"She'll be all right. I just know it."

"Yeah. But why . . . ? For some reason that's where my mind keeps going. It keeps wanting to ask why. Something about the setup of this, the timing, it feels almost evil."

"I know. I thought that, too."

Chapter 3

Opening her eyes, the early morning sun allowed Meg to see only the silhouettes of the various machines filling her hospital room. Mingled with the repetitious beeps of the monitors, she could hear the soft sound of Jadon's breath as it fell hard against her neck. Smiling, she absorbed the rhythm of his body as it worked to sustain him while he escaped into the world of exhausted sleep. As much as she wanted to look into his gentle blue eyes, she also wanted to feel him lying next to her, and listen to his breathing.

With the lulling music of Jadon's breath as the soundtrack for her thoughts, Meg realized she had made it back to him. Back to the place she longed to be. Not that she didn't want to be with her mother, but that place was not home, not yet. Instead, heaven lived within the few feet surrounding Jadon. And it had since the moment she first met him.

As if played by a movie reel suddenly un-jammed, the images of the other morning quickly spun free in front of Meg's mind. She could smell the ocean as it smelled that morning standing on the balcony, and she could see Jadon looking back at her. His eyes were full of love and relief that she was standing next to him, healthy and happy. As if her mind was no longer willing to keep secret the truth that forced her return to the hospital, Meg felt a stabbing pain shoot up her neck, and behind her ear. The pain, even if triggered only by a memory, caused her eyes to fill with tears.

I trusted you, God. Meg said to herself. *I trusted you. I gave in, and put my heart out there. Where are you now?*

Lifting his head slightly, Jadon listened to the monitors, noticing their rhythm had changed. He quickly glanced at Meg and saw her eyes looking into his.

⁓

John Hastings shut the door of his pickup truck, looked over at Larry and grinned. Larry's favorite perch was riding shot gun next to his owner. And John dutifully hoisted Larry's hefty, bulldog body in and out of his truck without exception every time he went anywhere — which wasn't often.

Reaching into the truck's storage compartment, John pulled out a flask of whiskey, and took a sip. Putting the truck into drive, he started down the long, winding road leading down the mountain and into the small Northern California town he had moved to after Jadon moved out decades ago.

As he sat alone on the first night after Jadon left, John vowed to never again live where the roofs all looked the same. Two weeks after, he sold the only home he had ever known and bought a small cabin on Cobb Mountain. Only rarely did he venture into town, and it was even rarer when he'd venture to the town he had once shared with Jadon's mother. Every time he did, he could still smell her perfume in the air. It was a sensation that brought back the pain of losing her, and sent him quickly back to his mountain cabin. And he wouldn't be venturing out now, except it had been too long since Jadon returned his calls.

John didn't share his emotions easily; he didn't know how. But that didn't mean he didn't possess them. The reality was that his emotions sat deeper than in most, hence the need to build such a thick wall around them. Giving Larry a rub on the head, John casually made his way onto

CA-29 and headed south toward Los Angeles, and thought about how it would feel to see his son for the last time.

⚬⚬⚬

Sitting cross-legged on her balcony, Flora watched as the sun brought light to a new day. As if a fire were burning beyond the trees, the sun made its appearance with a blaze. Watching the red glow burn behind the silhouette of trees, Flora felt a resonance with nature. It burned with possibilities while she burned with anger. Keeping her stare held steady on the emerging sun, she tried to see beyond the anger that held tight onto her spirit.

"Let go, Flora, just let go," she said, rotating her head trying to stretch her neck. "Let go."

Unable to do anything else, she dropped her head forward and cried.

"Hey, baby," Kofi offered gently, falling onto his knees behind her. Rubbing her shoulders softly, his eyes scanned her back as she released the angry tears that stabbed her soul. "Just let it out. Let it out. You won't be able to let anything new in, unless you let this out."

Kofi knew Flora like no one else. They had become partners shortly after he first walked into her yoga class when he was only in his mid twenties. Being already in her late thirties at the time, Flora resisted the attraction at first.

But then she came to realize his playful, delicate nature and youthful charm had nothing to do with age; they were part of his spirit: unchanging and permanent.

Kofi tried to comfort her while allowing her room to release all that rested inside her heart. Looking up, he watched as the sun moved steadily and swiftly into the sky, as if eager to get on with things and snap everyone out of their hazy slumber.

After time and energy had passed, with her head still hung low, Flora whispered, "Meg's awake. I'm almost positive. Meg's awake . . ."

⁕

With his face resting heavy in his hands, Stu didn't move until he recognized the pair of well worn sneakers that had stopped in front of him. His mind still humming from his frantic trip back to hospital once he received Chick's early morning call, he felt like he was enclosed in his own world, one where he could barely make out the sounds around him.

"Hey," Jadon said.

"I called Bob. He'll be here any minute," Stu said looking up and then behind Jadon. "That might be the rest of 'em."

Jadon spun around and watched the elevator doors open. Cemented in place, he scanned everyone until his gaze met Chick's face. Looking at Jadon, Chick didn't know if it was safe to smile. When Jadon called that morning he didn't say how Meg was, only that she had woken up. As he saw Jadon's eyes fill with tears, Chick felt his heart sink.

"Oh, God, don't tell me she isn't okay," Chick said.

Letting out a jagged sigh, Jadon shook his head. "No, it's not that. She's okay. I'm just still a little overwhelmed. I'm not sure if it's safe to breathe yet."

"Thank God!" Bob sighed.

"Can we see her?" Erin asked.

"Yeah, yeah. That's why I was waiting, so I could take everyone in. Where's Flora?"

"They were already on their way when I called, but they live further out, ya know. Might take them a bit longer," Stu answered, glancing at his watch.

Following Jadon, everyone walked down the long corridor of the hospital and into Meg's room. At the sound of shuffling feet, Meg opened her tired eyes. A small smile emerged on her face as she watched her new found family cautiously and anxiously fill the space surrounding her bed.

"Hey," Meg smiled.

"Hey, Meggie Peggie," Stu grumbled, trying to camouflage his faltering voice.

"You sure know how to get us worried," Chick said, trying to lighten his anxiety with humor.

"Well, I try," Meg said softly, giving a light chuckle.

Holding Meg's hand, Erin looked up at Jadon. "Well, what did Dr. Solomon say?"

"She's a fighter," Jadon started. "And she . . . has some side effects from the stroke. But she's going to be fine." Jadon nervously ran his hand through his long blonde hair.

"That's not *quite* what he said," Meg said, forcing a weak smile onto her face as she looked from Jadon to Erin.

"Well, I know Meg will be fine," Jadon insisted. "Doesn't matter what the doctor said. But, right now she has limited use of her right hand and arm. Other than that . . . I mean, considering, you know . . .considering what she just went through. It's a miracle."

Chick broke his gaze from Jadon to look at Meg. Feeling his eyes upon her, Meg turned and stared softly back. Chick could easily read what was written on Meg's mind, but didn't want to say it out loud. As if voicing her thoughts would bring them to life, transforming fears into permanent and tangible realities, Chick remained silent.

"I know what you're thinking," Meg said. "I don't know if I'll ever play again."

"It doesn't matter," Chick said quickly, his voice cracking. "What matters is that you're here."

"Yeah," Meg felt her words stop short. She couldn't give sound to what was in her heart and mind just yet. She couldn't travel down that road. Not even her normal armor of sarcasm could block the pain of not being able to play the violin. Even though from the very moment she felt her hand fail to respond to her first impulse to move it, it was the only road her mind wanted to travel.

Entering the room, Flora arrived with a gust of cool outside air still clinging to the long drapes of her skirt. Stopping at the foot of Meg's bed, Flora took a moment and looked intently at her.

Whether Meg knew it or not, she was the catalyst causing Flora to dig further within herself than she had ever gone before. And in doing so, Flora was penning volumes of questions along the way.

Why, can be a lethal word, often taking the mind into places it isn't strong enough to go. But looking at Meg, Flora could only ask, *why*. Why one person could be dealt so many hurdles and pain, when that very same person was kind and loving. Flora took her eyes from Meg's face and slowly scanned her right arm and hand.

"Meg, uh . . . can't move her right hand," Bob said softly, once he noticed where Flora's eyes ended their scan.

"She's going to be okay, right?" Chick asked quietly, hoping Flora could tap into her psychic abilities and give everyone, most of all Meg, a dose of hope.

"She will be all right," Jadon said, walking next to Meg's bed and taking her hand into his. "She will. I know it. I don't need anyone to look into the future. You know . . . I just know."

Looking up, Flora looked back into Meg's eyes. All she could see was pain.

Chasing Nirvana

Chapter 4

Opening the French doors leading to Meg's balcony, Jadon tried to bring fresh air into the house. As he looked around, he realized it had only been a week since Meg had been rushed to the hospital, but still he wanted to make sure things were just right before bringing her back home today. Erin was happy to sit with her while he stepped out. Even though Meg insisted she didn't need any company, Jadon was worried that, if given the opportunity, she would easily plummet over the edge once her mind settled onto the harsh reality of her condition. It was through the use of Meg's right hand that she expressed herself. For Meg, a right hand that lies dormant, is like a heart that stops beating. It was a scenario that Jadon didn't want to picture, as if somehow by picturing it, he would accidentally turn it into reality. Every time the images created themselves, he quickly replaced them with the image of Meg twirling her body effortlessly in the wind while standing on the cliff overlooking Mandalay Bay.

"Christ, should I wash the sheets? How often do you have to wash sheets?" Jadon mumbled to himself as he made his way over to the bedroom. He stopped to look into the kitchen and realized he needed to shop for food; once he did have Meg home, he didn't want to leave her.

He opened the door to the refrigerator just to confirm his suspicions, "Nothing. Wonderful," he grumbled, swinging the door closed.

Walking back into the living room, he stood quietly for a moment trying to remember what he was planning to do before he had decided to check the refrigerator.

"Must not have been important," Jadon said to himself walking out the door.

As he backed out of Meg's garage and onto the road, Jadon glanced toward his own house. Breaking hard, Jadon watched his father walk slowly but purposefully down the steps that led to his front door. As if sensing his son staring at him, John looked up.

~

"I know what you're trying to do," Meg smiled, looking at Erin with a lifted eyebrow.

"What?" Erin grinned, shifting her chair closer to Meg's hospital bed.

"You're trying to distract me from the fact that I will never be able to not only play the violin again but also write."

"No one said you won't ever be able to use your hand again, Meg." Erin put away the latest issue of *People* magazine she was hoping to distract Meg with. "No one has said that."

"I have."

"And I don't know why you say that."

Meg didn't want to answer; she looked out the window instead. Although she had an answer, even she didn't want to hear it. She didn't want to hear how she felt that God was gunning for her. How in every perfect situation, the bottom falls out. Some say life doesn't make sense, but in an odd way it did to Meg. Life is cruel and mean. Even when given something beautiful, it had tentacles of ugliness. The words rolling through Meg's mind were too vile to say, let alone think. Looking back at Erin, she gave her a soft smile of resignation. She wanted to think better thoughts, more hopeful thoughts, so she surrendered her mind for the moment, allowing Erin the opportunity to distract it.

"You look tired," Meg said.

"Well, it has been a rough couple of weeks, don't you think? Or should I say, a rough few months!" Erin laughed.

"No, it's more than that. Looking at you, it's like looking at the sun, still so bright, still so beautiful, but . . . tired, regardless of how bright it's shining."

"I'm good. Look at this . . ." Erin, wanting to change the subject, held open a magazine in front of Meg.

"There she is," Flora said, walking into Meg's hospital room. "Today's the big day, yes? So . . . tell me, what do we know?"

"Well, I can't speak for my tired friend here, but I happen to know without a doubt to never get into a cab in New York City alone," Meg replied." Might be that damn *Cash Cab*. I have discovered that I rarely make it beyond the twenty-five-dollar level on that damn show. So when I'm in New York, I need to travel in a pack. A very smart, well rounded intellectual pack."

"I take it you've been watching a good deal of TV during your stay," Flora said, sitting on Meg's bed.

"We also know that Jadon should be back in about an hour or so. He wanted to *freshen* up the house before Meg came home," Erin added, laughing at the way Jadon fussed over Meg.

"I see you two have retained your sense of humor," Flora said. "But what I'd like to know is, how you are?" She looked intently at Meg.

"I'm here. And . . . thankful for that," Meg answered, finding more fun in talking about the inane than her current health situation.

Something about Flora forced Meg to tune into her higher self, the self that knew better than to grumble and act like a child. Looking down at her right hand, Meg bit her lip, then glancing past Flora she tried to focus on the wispy clouds in the distant sky outside her window.

Flora looked at Erin and smiled. Erin smiled back, noticing Flora's face soften once she looked at her. It was a welcome change from the unsettled look Flora had been recently displaying.

"You need to get more rest," Flora told Erin.

"Seriously, you do look tired. Even Flora notices," Meg added.

"I'm good. Tired, but good. I slept like a rock last night. I'm good."

"You are good," Flora said. "But you still need more rest than you're used to. I'll sit with Meg. Go home. Take a nap. Doctor's orders." Flora motioned toward the door.

Erin nodded. She knew Flora was right. Standing at the doorway, she turned back toward Meg. "Once you're settled, I'm coming over. Love you."

"Love you, too."

Alone with Meg, Flora said, "Talk to me."

"What ya wanna know?" Meg said, harnessing a bit of her sarcastic tone.

Flora looked at Meg, but didn't answer. Meg's statement didn't hold within it any questions. It held only her pain.

"When you looked at me the other day, I know you saw something. You didn't say what, though. Which meant it was terrible. We're alone. Spill it," Meg paused, shifting her tone, revealing an unmasked vulnerability, "Please?"

"I saw pain, Meg."

"Oh, wonderful. God," Meg chuckled.

"Meg, there's something going on here. You have a purpose, but let me tell you, dear, you have to overcome some challenges before you're ready to move on."

"Purpose? What if I don't want a purpose? What if I don't want to do more than what I'm doing? I'm content for the first time in my life . . ."

"Are you? Really?"

"Well, yeah. Why wouldn't I be? I have everything. Or, I used to. Making music with Jadon . . . the band . . . writing . . . For the first time, I felt I had everything. I didn't even get to exhale yet, and so much of it was taken away. Why?"

"I don't have all the answers. But I think this was the only way possible. And a part of you knows that."

⌒

"Dad?" Jadon said, stepping out of his black Porsche and onto his driveway.

"Jay. Been a long time," John said, looking deep into his son's eyes and instantly noticing they were still just as blue as Jadon's mother's eyes had been, and still the polar opposite of his own. Jadon's eyes looked like cool, refreshing ocean water; John's looked like a moonless night.

"Yeah. It's been a long time, Dad. Why..?"

"Why am I here? Larry and I were about to take a road trip. Wanted to stop and see you first. Especially since you never return my calls." John cocked his head slightly before slipping his dark sunglasses back onto his well tanned, hardened face.

"I've been busy. I'm heading out right now, actually," Jadon said, not certain what to do with the situation. He didn't want to talk to his dad. He didn't want to see his dad. Plain and simple. "I, uh . . . I'm heading to the store. You want to come along, you can."

"Larry and I can wait here, Jay. Might be easier that way. I mean . . . if you're busy . . ." John turned to look back at Jadon's beach house, then back at his son.

"Hop in. Larry, too," Jadon said, stepping back into his car.

Looking at Larry then at his dad, Jadon wondered about the timing of his showing up. He then quickly questioned the reason for his showing up, knowing that his father hadn't ventured far out of his cabin except for a handful of times.

Shifting into reverse, Jadon glanced down at his hand resting on the shifter, and noticed how different it was from his father's hand that was resting on Larry. As he pulled into traffic, Jadon couldn't ignore the stream of thoughts that always flowed behind times spent with his father. They were different in every way. Jadon's skin was fair, his eyes soft blue. John was deeply tanned with eyes that appeared almost black. Jadon's hair was made of strands of every shade of blonde. John's hair was jet black except for the metallic gray dusting along his temples. Above all that, the feature that stood out furthest from the rest in Jadon's mind, and had since he first formed a memory of his father was that of his stature. John Hastings was a tall, wide wall of a man.

"A lot's happened since we last talked," Jadon said as they headed to town.

John nodded his head, but said nothing.

"I, uh . . . that's why I'm going to the store. I have to get some things before I pick up Meg from the hospital. Meg is . . . she . . ."

"I know who Meg is," John said calmly, while sliding Larry back onto his lap. "I don't know much, but I've seen some of the articles. The video. Your song. I've heard your song."

Jadon looked at his dad quickly, then back out the windshield.

"The news said she was back in the hospital," John continued.

"Uh . . . yeah, but she comes home today."

"And you love her." John made certain his words were a statement, not a question.

"Yes."

Every fiber in John's body knew what Jadon was feeling for Meg. The sound in his son's voice, the song he wrote; the look in his eyes. But as far as John was concerned, that type of love was like free-falling. There was no other way to experience it but to release one's self to it. Sometimes, if you're lucky, you glide. Sometimes, most of the time, you fall.

"This road trip, where are you going?" Jadon asked.

After all this time, it shouldn't matter what his dad did or thought. Yet, from some place deep inside, it still did. Years of trying to believe his dad no longer existed never accomplished anything except create a dark void inside Jadon's heart. But even that dark void felt better than reliving the memories he had. By making the word memory plural, Jadon hoped within somewhere in his mind it would diffuse the pain, like a million small bullets versus one large one. And as if, by focusing on the memories forged afterward, it would overshadow the one memory that changed him forever. The memory that lived liked a person, occupying life and space, not only between the two of them when he and his father were together but also within Jadon's mind whenever his mind drifted to thoughts of his father. No amount of smothering stopped the breath of the memory, nor was Jadon able to strangle the life out of it.

⤳

"Stop your Goddamn pacing," Stu barked, watching Chick walk the same circle repeatedly. "You're gonna wear a hole in the floor. Then when people come to the studio they'll fall through the fuckin' floor."

Chick stopped briefly to stare at Stu, then over at Bob, who didn't seem to care if he was pacing or not as he was too busy looking at the classifieds in the newspaper.

"Here's one!" Bob said, holding his finger on a classified ad. "Golden retriever puppies for sale."

"Are retrievers a good idea? Should we be thinking of a dog so like Bobby, or go completely in the other direction?" Chick asked, resuming his circular pace.

"She's gonna like anything we pick out. This is a good thing, as Martha would say," Stu said, lighting another cigarette. Stu didn't care if he'd been smoking more than normal. Lately his nerves were about as frayed as an old rug that'd seen too much traffic.

"Okay, well . . . did Jadon say what kind?" Bob looked up for a moment.

"Nah. He didn't care. He just wants us to find the perfect dog. Whatever the hell that is," Chick answered.

"Perfect dog. How about a pug?" Bob asked.

"Oh! I love pugs," Stu shouted. "Those are some screwy dogs. Maybe lookin' at a really goofy dog would help Meggie."

"A pug. A pug. I'm not feeling a pug. Keep looking," Chick said, snapping his gum.

"How 'bout we go to the shelter and rescue a dog?" Bob asked, tossing his pen onto the coffee table, and stretching his hands behind his head.

"Oh, man. Yeah. That sounds right. That feels right. Christ, just the thought of walking through there, though. All those sad eyes looking at me. God, I might take them all home," Chick said, throwing his hand onto his chest.

"They don't let you. They screen ya and everything before they let you take them home," Stu said.

"What? For real?" Bob questioned.

"Oh, yeah. They want to make sure you'll provide a good home," Stu said taking the last hit off his cigarette before snubbing it out in the ashtray on the table separating him from Bob.

"How the hell do you know?" Bob asked.

"That girl I was dating for a while, she wanted a dog for her kid, so . . ."

"Let's do it. Where's the shelter?" Chick interrupted.

Chapter 5

Devon,

I can't thank you enough for all your help and guidance. Arianna will make the perfect assistant for Meg, and I feel confident once I explain the need for her, Meg will be pleased that I hired her to assist with all her needs. Because you know Meg so well, I can easily see why Arianna makes the ideal fit. But as you requested, I will keep your contributions private.

~ Trish

Handle House Publishing

After reading the e-mail he received from Meg's new publisher, Devon slid his phone back into his coat pocket and relaxed into his chair. In a couple of hours the Hathaway corporate jet would be landing in New York, the first stop of many he had planned over the next few weeks.

Arianna had called early that morning and shared the news that Meg would be going home that day. And that's why both of them were currently crossing the Atlantic Ocean, steadily making their way in Meg's direction.

Although he didn't like parting with Arianna, his own personal assistant, he knew her talents would best be utilized working directly with Meg. And because Arianna had been working for him for only the past few weeks, Meg would never have heard of her.

Arianna knew she still worked for Devon, and he trusted she would honor his need for discretion. He carefully laid out her job duties: provide Meg with everything she needs, sparing no expense; gain her trust; gather every morsel of information she could; then report back to him. And from what he could tell, Arianna had no problem with the secrecy required.

Fortunately for Devon, Trish welcomed his help and never thought to question how graciously and freely he offered it. Or why he offered it.

Devon knew publishing. He knew the money involved and how desperately publishers needed success from their authors. If his assistance secured Meg's success at Handle House Publishing, he knew Trish would be indebted to him. And she was.

~

"Go. Just go!" Bob shouted, pointing toward the winding driveway leading away from the Bay City Animal Shelter.

"Christ, are they looking or something?" Chick asked frantically, looking over his shoulder past Stu and the motley dog seated next to him in the back seat of Erin's Jeep.

"I think I see them waving at us," Bob shrieked. "Keep going!"

"Jesus!" Chick shifted into gear and quickly bounded onto the road and away from the shelter.

Turning around Bob looked at Stu with an incredulous expression.

"What?" Stu let out a guttural laugh, while lighting a cigarette. "What ya lookin' at me like that for? I never said that was *our* dog crate. What did you think? Did ya think I suddenly wiggled my nose and a large dog crate just suddenly appeared?"

"Why the hell did you point at the crate then?" Bob shouted.

"Cause you asked if we had a crate, and they said we needed one. It was right there. So I pointed at the fucker. Who cares, we're gone now," Stu chuckled with satisfaction.

"We could have come back with one. Christ, I feel like outlaws on the run," Chick said, startled by their sudden escape from the animal shelter. "Everything was going along calm and smooth, then boom next thing I know we're throwing Perry in the Jeep and hauling ass out of there. They have my number, dumb ass. All they have to do is call. Christ, that's probably them now!" Chick shrieked shooting a quick look at his cell phone that was busy vibrating. "Thank God, just Erin. Hey, babe. Yeah . . . we got one. Perry. That was his name. He comes with a name already. He's like . . . five years old . . . Breed? Boxer. He's big too. Christ, takes up the whole backseat with Stu. Color? White."

Rubbing noses with the awkwardly large dog, Stu grinned. "How ya doin', Perry? Huh? Are you a good boy? Yeah, you're goin' do just fine," he said. "But I'm not sure about this name. Perry. It doesn't flow well. He needs somethin' that will fit that face of his. It doesn't sound tough enough. Kinda sounds like some prick."

"Well then how the hell is he going to know his name when we call him?" Bob asked. "He'll just sit there and look at us." Bob paused thoughtfully, then added, "We need to make certain he is relaxed before we hand him over to Meg, though. Maybe she isn't ready for such a large dog so soon after getting outta the hospital."

"The Perry man is staying with me for a while," Chick answered, snapping his gum nervously. "We'll make sure he's cool. Take him to the studio, have Jadon check him out.

He'll be good. Got to change the name though. I'm not liking the sound of Perry."

Sitting at a red light, Perry let out a bark that became a howl, then turned to look directly at Stu as if for approval.

"Watcha' lookin' at? There a girl over there? Huh? You like rock music, Perry? Cause you're gonna be surrounded by it, my friend," Stu said, wrapping his arm around Perry. "How about Larry? I like Larry."

Jadon held Meg close and tried to breathe. He knew too well what it felt like to have a thief take away the one you love. And he couldn't escape the haunting feeling that there was an invisible intruder trying to find its way into their lives to steal the very thing that meant the most to him: Meg.

Looking at the ocean that rolled methodically back and forth just beyond the French doors that opened into her bedroom, Meg took a deep breath, and let the warm, salty air fill her lungs. In doing so, she remembered the first time she noticed the intoxicating aroma that occupied the spaces around her home. She was standing in her driveway. She and her Irish setter were about to begin writing the next chapter of their lives in Bay City. Even though the sentences about to be written were unknown to her, she couldn't shake the eerie feeling that surrounded them. Almost as if there was a hidden climax to the story waiting to reveal itself. Watching the forceful waves rush onto the beach before being magnetically pulled away, Meg tried to absorb the story that unfolded within the pages of that chapter, and wondered if the worst was behind her, or yet to come.

"I could lie here forever," Jadon said, curling tightly behind Meg on her large white bed. "In fact, that should be the plan."

"I like that plan," Meg smiled, looking over her left shoulder at him while he softly kissed her bare skin. "You said you were sidetracked for a bit before getting me at the hospital. What happened?"

Meg's question caused Jadon to pause for a moment before resuming what he enjoyed, rather than talking about something he didn't. Resting his forehead on Meg's shoulder, he tried to gather his thoughts.

"I discovered my dad standing on my steps earlier," Jadon said, not lifting his head.

"Oh. For reasons I'm unsure of, this sounds like a bad thing."

"Well, to me it is."

Wanting to look at Jadon, Meg turned on her back. The few words he was revealing weren't telling her enough; she needed visual clues as well.

"Where is he now?" she asked.

"At my place, with Larry."

"Who's Larry?"

"A big ass bulldog that goes everywhere he goes," Jadon answered, turning over to rest his head on the pillow next to Meg.

Lying quietly beside Jadon, Meg realized for the first time that despite how naturally connected she felt with Jadon, and despite all they'd gone through, there was very little she knew about him. All she knew about his family was that he was an only child and his mother had died while he was young. And of course, Meg remembered, Jadon's father bought him a piano for Christmas. The thought of that made her smile and question how bad his father could be. When her parents had given her a violin, it was done with love.

Meg stared at Jadon's profile and ran her fingers across his beard and onto his lips. "Remember that night at the camp site, right before the accident, when everyone shared their thoughts on heaven? You said something about how after your mother died your dad was never the same. What did you mean by that?" she asked slowly, certain it was a loaded question despite how innocent it appeared.

Jadon exhaled deeply before looking at Meg. "It's . . . my dad and I . . . we just don't do well together."

Scanning his face, Meg wondered if she should ask him to go further. As Jadon turned his head toward hers, she smiled a soft, safe smile, as if her body wanted to confirm what her mind hoped he already knew. Whatever memories he had, whatever secrets might be resting deep inside him, would be kept safe.

Jadon knew he needed to tell her all he could, and he wanted to. The memories of his father, and of his childhood, were like images held within a scrapbook he had purposely never shared with anyone, ever. Some of the details he wished he could simply rip out of the book and throw away, destroying them forever. Maybe, though, he wondered if they would vanish not by shelving them in the back corner of his mind but by showing them. And there was no one he felt safer with than Meg. When she played her violin on her balcony those many nights, she wasn't the only one releasing dark memories.

"My mom died when I was young. You knew that, right? She died . . . of a heart attack," Jadon rubbed his face with his hands. "She was only thirty-five. I was . . . twelve. It happened just like that," he said, snapping his fingers. "It blew my dad away. No one saw it coming. She wasn't doing anything weird, either. It was a nice morning, and they were working in the yard. She told him she didn't feel good. She felt tired, and she thought maybe she was getting sick. She didn't have even one chest pain. He said that she thought she was getting hit hard with the flu all the sudden. He took her in the living room. She stretched out on the couch and said she needed to rest. She just kept feeling worse, he said. When she said she felt like she couldn't breathe he ran to the phone, but within minutes, she went into full cardiac arrest. He watched it. He called for help, but . . . they couldn't get to her in time. Her eyes opened, she stared at him. Then she was gone. Right before his eyes. He couldn't do a thing to save her. He didn't even know what was going on."

"Where were you?" Meg whispered.

"I wasn't even home. I missed the whole thing. That morning I jumped on my skateboard and went to hang out at a friend's house. It was a beautiful Saturday morning. No reason to stay home. When my dad called and told me to come home . . . when I did, I didn't just lose my mom, I lost my dad, too. Because that man sitting on the front steps when I rolled into the driveway wasn't my dad."

Meg leaned in and kissed his face. Rubbing her cheek against his she wiped away the tears falling from his eyes.

"It's okay," she said. "It was the worst day imaginable for both of you, I have to believe."

"No. Almost, but seeing you floating in the river. That . . . that was the worst sight I could ever see. That night when you slipped away. I thought you were gone. That was the worst day."

Hugging him with her left arm, she held him tight. "Well we made it. Opening my eyes in the hospital and seeing you, that was the best day ever," she smiled. "Sounds like your dad was lost pretty bad."

"Yeah, well . . . he never was a softie. I mean, God, he was a police detective all of his life. He killed guys when he had to. I mean, he was tough. Big and tough. But something about my mom, she . . . she was able to bring out this side of him. And that's the side I guess I grew up with, until she died. I don't know. He tried though. He tried to create something between us, but . . . the love wasn't there. Can't show something if it isn't there in the first place." Jadon stopped. Pausing, he looked at Meg and then off into the room, trying to hold back the tears and anger that wrapped around the memory he knew he was about to relive.

"Why do you say that? I mean . . ."

"This one time, it told me all I needed to know. It explained everything. His distance."

"What happened?" Meg asked, keeping her cheek rested against his.

"This one morning he woke me up and told me we were going for hike. I didn't want to. But, we were doing a lot of arguing, I don't know, maybe he thought it would bring us closer. All it did was throw us worlds apart. Of course we couldn't go hiking on one of the millions of hiking trails scattered all over the county, no . . . not John Hastings. No, we headed off into the woods. I didn't care. I just walked behind him and wanted the day to be over. I don't know what I was thinking. I was off in my own world. But I saw this metal pipe sticking out of the ground. I ran over to see what it was. My dad was already way ahead of me. I started yanking on this old rusted pipe. Suddenly the ground under my feet just disappeared. I must have been standing on some old wooden well covering. And with me jumping around on it, it gave way. There I was, hanging on for dear life, screaming my head off. It was deep. I couldn't see the bottom and the rocks that were falling around me took forever to hit bottom. I wasn't like at the top hanging on. I was already down a few feet into the hole with my fingers wrapped around this big root coming out of the ground. I couldn't pull myself up at all. I was scared to death."

Pulling herself up, Meg was gripped by the story he was sharing and what happened next. Whatever it was, she knew it wasn't good. The tears rolling from his eyes didn't look like tears of joy. Instead they looked like tears of pain. Scanning his face with her eyes, Meg wondered in amazement for a moment. Lying in front of her was the most beautiful color of love. A person who, like her, was a soul wrapped in pain from losing someone. And just like her pain, Jadon's pain was held deep within. Meg knew that the pain living at the deepest depths of the soul was always the most vicious. As if the animal grew larger the further down it went.

"What happened..," Meg whispered.

"What happened next? Well . . . ha," Jadon let out a soft, painful chuckle. "My dad showed up. He must have been running hard because he was out of breath. He threw himself down on his knees and was about to reach down for me. Then he stopped. He stopped, Meg, and stared. Just looked me square in the eye and didn't move. You know how sometimes you can almost tell what someone is thinking . . . looking into his eyes, I could tell he was deciding if he should save me or let me go."

Erin searched the house from room to room looking for Chick, then headed toward the garage, only to hear the sound of an angry guitar the closer she walked. Opening the door, she found Chick, busy releasing his frustrations onto his guitar. His tall, thin body moved violently as he threw his hand hard across the strings. As if taking the place of the drums, each long dark strand of hair whipped back and forth to the steady beat his body was sending out. Leaning her body against the door frame, Erin smiled at what she was watching. Chick's long body looked in many ways the same as it did when they first met.

"Haven't heard you play like that in a long time," Erin said, looking at Chick with a warm smile as he spun around. "Angry . . . gritty rock, with a hint of punk angst. That style always did suit you. If I remember correctly, that's the music you were wearing when we first met."

"I was angry *then*, too. Just for different reasons. I was broke and couldn't get anyone to take me or my music seriously." Chick paused for a moment, shook his head and leaned his guitar against its amp. "I'm playing the same damn way now, only now they call me a genius. Hell, what was I when they said I had no talent and wouldn't amount to anything?"

"To get the music to the ones who'll appreciate it, you first have to go through the ones who don't. You know that. But we did okay; we've made it this far. So, what's bringing out the anger now?" Erin slid her body onto the stool next to him.

Chick let out a disgusted snort. "Don't forget, they put you up high, half hoping you'll fall."

"Where's this all coming from?" Erin repeated.

"Meg. Meg, I guess. Christ. How can anyone make sense of that situation? It's fucked. God," Chick said, letting his tired head fall to the side while he grabbed the pack of Lucky Strikes from his shirt pocket before sliding his stool closer to Erin. "And I can't let go of it."

"You gonna let me hear it then?"

"It's rough still. But, it's right. It's already got good form. Good bones."

"The best songs are a bit rough," Erin smiled.

"Well . . . when I was letting this flow out, man, I felt a whole new vibe come on. Actually, an old vibe. But, I think right now, maybe I need to focus in a different direction. The acoustic work is on hold. Maybe forever. If Meg doesn't . . . ," Chick paused.

"She will. She'll recover."

"We don't know that. Everything feels up in the air and completely fucked up. I don't even want to touch the acoustic stuff unless she's standing on my left side, right where she's supposed to be."

"She's so worried about letting everyone down. She said she tells her hand to move and it won't. She can't write, she can't play violin. She can't do anything with it. And I don't know how she is handling that. I know Jadon feels she will get full use back, but . . . I'm worried, too. Not because of the music. But for her. Writing and making music is like breathing for Meg. And that's the obvious truth that sits on everyone's face as they look at her . . . and she looks at them. And it's horrible," Erin said, wiping a tear from her cheek.

"Come here." Chick pulled Erin tight against him. "I know. I feel like life is this beautiful place. Like a hillside with wildflowers, birds, intoxicating fruit and sunny skies, but it's peppered with land-mines. Some people, without even knowing it, walk around them. Others, like Meg and Jadon, keep stepping on them. Dead on. And it doesn't make sense."

"God, I'm tired," Erin said into Chick's ear.

"Flora said you need to rest more. You feeling all right? I'm starting to wonder about you. You're never *this* tired," he said, pulling his head back to look Erin in the eye.

"Other than feeling as though I'm drained to the bone of any possible energy, I feel fine," Erin smiled, giving Chick a tender kiss.

"That still doesn't sound right to me. Tomorrow I'm calling your doctor. Is that okay? You'll let me do that, right?"

"Yeah. I'll let you do that," Erin grinned, grabbing Chick's arm and turning off the light in the garage.

Chapter 6

Holding the phone to her ear, Meg remained silent as she listened and looked out the window at the ocean. "All right. Sure, that sounds good. No, you're right. I do need the help. Yeah, that will make a big difference. I appreciate it, thank you. I know, yeah . . . three weeks till the first interview. How could I forget?" She paused, casting a quick glance across the kitchen to Jadon. "Uh, no. I've never used Facebook or Twitter. Okay, I can do that. Okay, thank you."

Putting the phone on the kitchen counter, Meg turned and released a chest full of nervous energy.

"Who was that," Jadon asked, pouring two cups of coffee, "Trish?"

"Yeah . . . she said she's sending an assistant to help me. Someone to do all that I can't . . . do," Meg said, relieved but frustrated. Even though she knew an assistant was a good thing, she couldn't shake the feeling that came with the thought of needing one. "She also said I have to set up a Facebook page and MySpace. She asked if I use Twitter. God, I don't do any of those things. Can't say I really want to either. All of this, it just feels so complicated now that . . ."

"Now that Devon isn't handling it, you mean?" Jadon asked gently, as he carefully handed Meg her cup of steaming coffee.

Taking a deep sigh, Meg wasn't sure she knew how to answer. "Maybe. But . . . I can do this."

"I know you can," Jadon said. "I'm glad this assistant is coming, though. Because I don't know a thing about publishing. I'm going to be there every step of the way. But I'm just not sure where those steps are going."

Noticing her left hand was beginning to shake from nerves, Meg slowly put the cup down on the counter. Wrapping her left hand around her right arm, she walked out onto the balcony. She stared at the waves; watching as they held steady to their mission, their orders called out by the invisible pull that guided them. The waves knew what to do, deviating only in the size and shape they chose.

Meg, too, always felt she had a mission. From a very early age she knew she wanted to be a writer. More than that, she knew she was meant to be a writer. Yet, the very one who called out the invisible orders had also taken away her ability to write.

Placing her right hand onto the thick, white balcony railing, Meg stared at it, a hand that responded more like a stranger's than that of her own. With her left hand she carefully traced each finger on her lifeless right hand, feeling the touch on every finger. *God, why can't I get my hand to move?* Meg wondered.

Hearing Jadon's footsteps behind her, Meg said with an unhappy chuckle, "Her name is Arianna."

"Sounds okay, I guess." He could already tell that nothing about the assistant was going to sit right with Meg.

"Sounds young." Meg slammed her left hand onto her right hand.

"Meg! Don't do that. I know you're upset. But . . . look at me. We're going to get through this. All of it. The whole big, fucking mess."

Holding her right arm tight to her chest, Meg looked into his eyes. Life was a mess. And the mess wasn't just hers anymore. It was a shared mess. Letting out a soft smile at the thought, Meg couldn't help but to feel blessed. It was ironic, but she couldn't help but feel good somehow. Her life had always been a journey walked alone. Her days were without complications, not easy, but not challenging either. The only difficult part was the struggle to ignore the loneliness and pain of losing her parents. Now she was standing in a place, having caught up with and living within the dream she crafted years prior. Never once though had she imagined the mess that would accompany the dream.

"What . . . what is it?" Jadon whispered, leaning his head to get a better view of the subtle disbelief that rested on Meg's face.

"This. My stroke. All that Dr. Solomon told us . . . my condition . . . Bobby . . . Devon . . . your dad . . . the book — all of it." Meg smiled as her face tightened with tears. "But then, there's you. And all those years ago when my heart cried out for someone, for you, I never would have imagined all these other things. Yet, I have you now. So, part of me is still so happy."

Jadon held Meg's face in his hands and kissed her tears. Resting his forehead against hers, he said, "I know. I want to take you away. I want a moment just for us. Instead it feels like we skipped past the getting to know each other part. But . . . I still wouldn't trade any of it, if it means not having you."

Meg let the full weight of everything wash over her while Jadon held her face steady in his hands. For the first time she shared her grief. This time her grief embodied more than the loss of her parents. Now it included the loss of so much more. In Meg's mind, she lost her ability to be what Jadon fell in love with. She lost her ability to do what she was born to do: write and play music. Everything that ripped inside of Meg's heart, every sharp thought, she released while Jadon held her.

As her cries lessened, she began to take full, deep breaths of the salty ocean air. Jadon held her hand and led her back into the house. Looking back at her, he stopped to wipe her tears from her face then kissed under her eyes. He took her hands in his, walked to the bedroom, carefully laid Meg down on her bed, and brought his body tightly beside hers.

As they lay silently together, he ran his fingers through her hair. As it always did, time suspended itself while he stared into her eyes. Taking the lengthened moments given to him, Jadon ran his fingertips softly over Meg's body. Brushing his lips over Meg's right arm, he looked up at her, smiled and whispered, "Do you feel that?"

"Yes," Meg answered, her eyes flowing again with tears.

"That's because it's a part of you. It is you. And I love you. Every inch. I love this beautiful arm, and these magnificent fingers, just as much as I love the ones on your left hand. Just as much as I love your sensual lips, and your deep, mysterious eyes. Because it all belongs to you, Meg."

As she attempted to respond, her voice faltered, submerged under a wave of emotions. Jadon pulled himself up to look her in the eye and brought his mouth onto hers. Keeping his fingers nested in her hair, he cradled her head in his hands, brought her head toward his, and pushed his mouth deeper into hers.

Sliding his head between Meg's breasts and down her stomach, Jadon smelled her skin and tasted her body as it responded to his touch. Carefully, he brought his body delicately into her, and her body tight against his where they remained motionless. With his forehead resting against Meg's, he wanted to feel her. He wanted his body and mind to absorb as much of her as was possible. Knowing once he began to move, his desire to consume her would prevent him from taking the time to feel her heart beating beneath his. For as long as he could, he wanted to be still in the moment, one with her.

Nudging her mouth open with his lips, he looked deep within Meg's eyes, "God, I love you," he whispered into her mouth as he closed his eyes.

As he ran his hand down the small of her back, Meg arched her body tighter into his. Jadon smiled and tilted his head slightly to the side. "Promise me this," he whispered, "promise me . . . when it's our time to go, we'll die together."

"Promise," Meg smiled, pulling his mouth back onto hers.

⸙

Much like the countless crime scenes he'd encountered during his career, John walked cautiously throughout Jadon's living room, memorizing every detail. Stopping at the bookshelf, he noticed the small photo album that used to sit next to his wife's side of the bed. After she died, he gave it to Jadon and hadn't seen it since. John gently touched its leather cover, then held his hand on the small book before finally sliding it off the shelf.

Walking out onto the balcony, he eased his tired body onto one of the chairs facing the ocean. He stared at the blank cover of the photo album and took a moment to prepare himself for what was inside. As he opened the first page John felt his heart tighten.

"Emily," John whispered, looking at the faded photo of Jadon's mother holding her newborn son. "God, you were so happy. What a day that was."

Closing his eyes, John's mind instantly brought back that February day thirty-seven years ago. He could smell the hospital. He could smell his sweat exactly as it was that day while he raced through the hall trying to find Emily's room. He could see the look in her expansive, blue eyes as he flung the door open only minutes before she was taken away to deliver Jadon. Despite the pain, and the uncertainty, her face glowed with hope. Emily was born to be a mother, and that day was her dream coming true. And John couldn't have been happier. Knowing she was happy, and that he'd helped to make her that way, was all he needed.

Turning the page, John ran his finger across the photos, which after all these years remained perfectly in place. He remembered watching Emily carefully glue each photo mounting corner onto the page and then tuck each picture into place.

As his eyes scanned across the images, his mind scanned through the years. Every milestone was captured. Emily made certain not to miss one major event, and hardly any minor ones, either. Looking at the photos, John could still feel Emily's love for him. She was indebted to him because he gave her Jadon. John was indebted to her, because she gave him her love.

"Look at you, Em, holding Jay's hand while he took his first steps," he said softly, turning the pages. "Remember when he blew out those candles? He nearly blew the cake over." John chuckled painfully. "There you are, Em, so proud that Christmas. We managed to get him a new skateboard and that used drum set. God, I worked a lot of overtime so we could pay for those drums. Remember how you had to talk me into getting them? Your convincing paid off, Em.

You'd be proud. You'd be real proud of what he's done."

Happiness wasn't what John felt, yet his face knew only to smile as he remembered every moment and how Emily had celebrated each one. Taking a minute to let his dark eyes clear, John looked out at the water. Years ago he convinced himself there were no more tears left to cry, yet there always were. Like a natural spring, the tears refused to stop flowing.

After she died, he committed himself to not think of her. It was the only way to keep his mind held together. He worked overtime and double shifts. As a cop, he found it easy to hide behind distractions. Life always provided wrongs needing to be set right.

Letting one hand fall onto Larry's head, John slowly turned each page with the other until he stopped and took in every detail of a photo of Emily as she sat on the hillside behind their house. He remembered the moment. He remembered it well. She was watching Jadon set up a skateboard jump on the driveway. John was supposed to be snapping pictures of Jadon once he hit the ramp, but seeing Emily sitting so happy and content, he had to capture that image. Of course he could never have imagined then that, within months of that moment, he would be without her. The picture was faded, but the memory was vivid and her blue eyes still made it hard for him to look away.

"I'm coming, Em," John whispered, closing the album. "I'm coming."

Chapter 7

"How's she doing?" Chick asked into the cellphone, as he sat on the sofa at the studio, one hand holding the phone, the other rubbing Perry's white head. "Erin told me yesterday . . ."

"She's . . . all right. One moment real good. The next . . . well, ya know, not so good. Her checkup went well. Some good news, some . . . not so good," Jadon said, pacing on his balcony. "It's like we can't quite move ahead. Everything is just suspended."

"She met the infamous John Hastings yet?"

"No," Jadon glanced into his house to see where his dad had gone.

"Eventually she's going to have to."

"I suppose so. I'm over at my place now, just checking on things. I might be able to avoid it. He said he'll be leaving tomorrow. God, I hope so."

"What did Dr. Solomon say, anyway?" Chick asked while at the same time examining Perry's ears.

"The good news is they can't see any real reason why Meg doesn't have use of her arm. The tests show that she should actually have full use. But, she can't move it at all. So, I don't know if that means it's something more serious and we just need to keep testing. Or, she'll suddenly start moving her arm and hand."

"Do you think you can come over to the studio? We got the little dude you asked for," Chick said with a snap of his gum.

"Yeah. I'll just double check on my dad and then head your way." Jadon ended the call and opened the balcony door. "Dad?"

Looking quickly around his house, Jadon realized his dad must have taken Larry for a walk. When he returned to the living room, he also noticed everything was exactly as he had left it. Nothing, it appeared, had been touched or moved. Judging by appearances, it was as if his dad had never been there.

❧

Meg slid the sofa pillow off her face and sat up in an attempt to gain her senses. Listening to the doorbell ring again, her mind began to click.

"Oh, God, that better not be Arianna. Christ, she's not supposed to show up till later," Meg mumbled, looking at the clock as she walked toward the door.

Swinging the door open abruptly, Meg stepped back, and looked up.

"You must be Meg," John said in a low steady voice while unintentionally giving Meg a peculiar grin.

Standing in front of Jadon's father, Meg understood instantly what Jadon had meant when he said his dad looked nothing like him. Instead of voicing a polite reply, she let her eyes take in this person who, until Jadon's recent revelations, was a total mystery. Everything she had heard of him thus far, made her heart quicken as she stared at him.

He looked as though he had spent most of his life bronzing under the sun. His face told of a life rich from experience and, sadly, turmoil. John Hastings' black hair reflected the sunlight as brilliantly and as purposely as the silver strands that framed his temples. And it was obvious that his large, dark eyes were taking advantage of the opportunity given to him, as he absorbed the woman who captured his son's heart like Jadon's mother had captured his. Meg couldn't help but notice the fact that his all-black outfit only added to his formidable appearance.

"And you must be Jadon's father. I'm sorry for thinking so slowly. Please come in," Meg said.

"Thank you. Do you mind if . . .?" John asked, turning slightly to motion toward the bulldog waiting patiently behind him.

"Oh, no, not at all. I don't mind. I love dogs. The more the merrier," Meg smiled, holding the door open for Larry to amble in slowly behind John.

"By chance, is my son here?"

"No, Jadon ran to the studio. I'm told they're working on a *surprise*," Meg said with a soft laugh as she motioned to one of the chairs in the kitchen. "Would you like to sit down?"

John paused and thought for a moment. He had something else on his mind, but the opportunity to learn more about Meg was too tempting of an offer to refuse.

"I just might. I just might," John said, pulling out one of the four chairs surrounding the small glass table.

"Can I get you anything?" Meg waved her hand toward the fridge, "I could make . . . I mean . . ." She paused and shook her head in frustration. "I could *try* to make coffee. A drink? We have wine. Oh, well, I can't do that either, it seems. The cork. Takes two hands."

Meg could easily see her own nervousness, and she was pretty certain so could Jadon's father. Nothing about him should make her nervous, but what Jadon had shared regarding him was so enthralling that Meg couldn't help but to feel unsettled. She also couldn't help but wonder if Jadon was right, if his father did have to think twice before saving him.

Taking a seat next to John, Meg decided that if ever she had been a criminal, and been brought in by Jadon's father, she wouldn't have stood a chance. She would've cracked on the spot. His imposing presence alone was enough to make her confess to things she hadn't even done, let alone things she had.

"If all we need are two hands, then we're just fine. I count three that can get the job done, which means we have one to spare," John said, with a smile that took even him by surprise.

Meg's eyes brightened. She thought how interesting it was that John's face transformed so completely when he smiled. Opening the wine cooler, Meg scanned the few bottles of wine she had, and grabbed a Pinot Noir.

"I don't really care for the whites. Hope you don't mind," Meg said.

Using the corkscrew Meg handed him, John effortlessly pulled the cork out, and handed the bottle to her. Within seconds Meg had two wine glasses filled and waiting for them on the table.

"Suppose we should let them breathe, but...," Meg laughed quietly at herself. "I'm more concerned about it helping me to breathe."

John took a sip while keeping an eye on Meg. Jadon had given him a rough run down of Meg's condition and prognosis, but hadn't shared anything about her as a person. Still, John knew the basics and perhaps a bit more.

"So, you hear from Devon anymore?" John asked.

"Whoa. Where'd that come from?" Meg said surprised, prompting her to take another drink. "Wonder if I can drink yet?" she said, whispering more to herself than to her guest. Her question was of only mild concern, her main concern was how to change the topic of conversation.

John waited patiently for Meg to answer. He realized the question seemed abrupt. But, in asking it in the way he did, he knew Meg's response would provide far more information than what her words alone could ever say.

"No. Not anymore. He used to call and e-mail. A lot. Every day actually. But . . . no. He sort of fell off the face of the earth while I was recovering." Meg wondered why he would ask such a thing but tried to shrug it off, figuring that Jadon must have discussed more than she had guessed with his father.

"Just stopped contacting you completely?"

"Yeah. Poof. Gone. Which is good. Don't have to worry about him anymore."

John stared at Meg then took another drink. He didn't like her answer. As soon as she gave it, his stomach took an abrupt flip.

"And why do you think that?" he asked.

"Why do I think I don't have to worry about him? I guess because he's gone," Meg answered, thinking the reason was obvious.

Leaning his elbows on the table, John rested his fingers on the base of the wine glass and slowly began sliding it on the table, making perfectly shaped circles with every motion.

"Meg, when it comes to a threat, such as Devon, you worry when they're gone, not when they're in plain sight," John said, keeping his head held in the direction of his glass, while his eyes moved toward Meg.

"I think Devon has moved on. I'm with a new publisher now, and he knows what he did. The damage he caused. He knows how I feel," Meg said, swallowing hard.

She wasn't expecting the conversation to instantly turn so personal, and so uncomfortable. Not knowing if she should keep the spotlight turned on her, or if she should turn it in a different direction, Meg tried to think of another subject.

"You know, while you're in town, maybe you could help me move some of Jadon's things over here. I mean, I think he would like that. I want him to know this is his home, as much as it is mine. Maybe some pictures. Something," Meg said nervously. "Heck, I didn't even know what you looked like until you showed up today, and you're his dad. I know his mother passed away. I'm sorry for that . . . for your loss. I haven't even seen a photo of her. Maybe he'd like to have some around . . ."

Slowly, John leaned forward and slid his wallet from his back pocket. Opening the faded, black leather that carefully protected all he chose to put in it, John pulled out a photo of Jadon's mother and slid it toward Meg.

Picking up the photo, Meg stared in astonishment.

"My God. Jadon and his mother look so much alike. It's amazing. Their eyes especially." Meg looked over at John then back at the photo. "She's . . . stunning."

John nodded, but said nothing. Instead he watched Meg as she took in every detail of Emily. John felt his heart twist with pain as he watched her. He wanted to talk about Jadon's mother, but couldn't. Not without losing himself. So he remained silent; the only movements he offered were grateful eyes. He hadn't shared Emily's picture with anyone since she died. Now, he was glad to share her beauty with someone who, to his son, was just as beautiful.

Watching Meg's eyes carefully memorize the photo, he noticed her youthful glow, despite how life had tried to age her. Not only were his senses as a detective engaged from what she had told him about Devon, but also his heart was softened and drawn to Meg.

"Her name is Emily, right?" Meg looked up briefly. "I'd like to have a picture of her here. Something in her eyes. They make me feel . . . I don't know." She paused, suddenly aware that her eyes were tearing up. "They make me feel kind of like, it'll be all right."

"I am also sorry for your loss, Meg," John said.

Meg looked up, startled that Jadon's father would know yet another detail about her life, this time a very intimate one.

John grinned and answered the question he read in Meg's eyes. "Jadon's my only child. I watch over him. Even from afar."

"Oh, yeah. I guess you are probably very good at getting background checks on people . . ." Meg let her words trail off, still not sure how she felt about his knowing her parents were gone without her having told him. "Why'd you ask about Devon?"

"I don't care for him," John answered easily.

Meg nodded her head. She didn't care for him either after all he had done to her and, most of all, the hell he had put Jadon through.

"Meg, Devon is the kind of person you need to keep an eye on. People are fires. Some burn in balance, efficiently and with purpose, just as they are meant to. Others are like a house on fire. Eventually they burn to the ground. Devon, I believe, is a house on fire, and I don't want you or Jadon trapped in the house when the last timber falls."

Looking out the picture window in her kitchen that displayed the ocean as the masterpiece it was, Meg considered John's words. *Let him burn then*, she thought.

"Then there are people like me, who have a bum match," Meg snickered, picking up her glass and taking another sip.

"Is that how you see yourself?"

"I can't even *strike* a match right now, John. So, yeah, that's how I see it," Meg said, not hiding her bitterness. "Can't burn efficiently or in balance when you're stuck with a piece of wet wood."

And that's the fire, John said to himself, *that's the right kind of fire.* Not that he liked to see the pain Meg was going through. He did, however, like to see her fire, knowing it was that very same fire that would eventually cause the wet wood to burn.

"I think you'll end up surprising yourself." John slid out his chair. "I'd like to do this again, Meg. Thank you."

Standing up quickly, Meg looked up with a smile. "I would like that. Very much. Will you be in town much longer?"

John paused before answering. "I think I will. I believe there's a couple things I need to take care of before I go."

⋙

Opening the door to the studio, Jadon found Chick and Stu reclined on the sofa, separated by a large white dog.

"Hey!" Stu shouted. "Come here! We got someone you need to meet. Jadon meet Larry; Larry, this is Jadon."

Jadon smiled and knelt down in front of Larry. "Wow, he is gorgeous. In a very . . . ah, unique way. I mean, that face. He looks like he's fed up with things."

"Yeah, he looks like he's down-right pissed. I like that." Stu beamed like a proud parent.

Chick shot off the sofa and smacked his leg, motioning for Larry to follow him.

"We got him trained pretty good. For a day or so we had to use his old name. We thought the new one was close enough that he wouldn't notice, but . . . we were wrong," Chick said, bending down to examine Larry's face, as he often did.

"You should have heard us. We sounded like fucking idiots walking around, 'Come here Larry Perry, come here Larry Perry.' We looked like dipshits. Thank God he finally caught on," Stu snorted.

Jadon threw himself down on the chair across from Stu and motioned for Larry to come over. Larry looked at Chick, then at Jadon. Chick nodded, letting Larry know it was all right.

"Uh oh, looks like he's already attached," Jadon said, giving Larry a rub down.

"We considered that," Chick said, rubbing his beard. "But I think he's just a damn good dog. Smart, too. Freaky smart."

"Yeah, we caught the little fucking bandit in the fridge the other day!" Stu shot a thumb out behind him directed toward the small refrigerator nestled in the corner of the studio.

Using the time to rub Larry as therapy for himself, Jadon began to relax. Stu and Chick noticed the tired expression that settled quickly onto Jadon's face.

"How's Meggie Peggie getting around?" Stu asked.

"Good. She can't wait to see everyone tomorrow," Jadon said, not looking away from Larry's steady gaze.

"When is her assistant supposed to show?" Chick asked.

"Day after tomorrow. She's not looking forward to it. I think she's not liking all of the upcoming publicity obligations she has. I know it's because she doesn't feel ready, because of the stroke. But I also get a feeling she almost regrets writing under her own name. I wonder if she regrets changing publishing companies?" Jadon looked up at Chick. "You know Devon would have swooped in and just moved heaven and earth for her to make all this effortless and oh so easy. I can't do anything. I don't even know what someone does when they promote a book. Hell, I can't help her in that way. I can be there, but . . . she needs more than that. And I don't have a fucking clue." He sank back into the chair.

"Fuck it. We'll figure it out. And this assistant, she'll help. Hell, that's what she's paid to do," Stu said, frustrated for Jadon. Also, the mere mention of Devon's name still made Stu boil with anger.

"Yeah, the acoustic stuff is on hold, dude. If we can't go on stage together to play it, all of us, then it's on hold. I'm working on some other stuff, but we'll hammer that out in between helping Meg. If we're all there, she can't fail. Even if we're just standing around like dorks, we're her dorks," Chick smiled, grabbing a cigarette and giving it a quick light.

"When is the therapist coming over?" Stu asked.

"He's been coming over. Nothing's working so far. It's like we're all looking at a pet rock, hoping to hell it will get up and walk." Jadon sighed and sank deeper into the chair.

"Chick's got a new song he's been messin' with," Stu said, motioning toward Chick.

Jadon shot a quick look at Chick. He was always excited about the next thing to flow from Chick when the urge hit him to write. Often, the song would take the band in a slightly altered direction.

"I want to hear it. Got a few riffs to share?" Jadon asked.

"More than that. Hell, he's got the whole damn song chiseled into place. Why ya being a modest mouse over there?" Stu said, flicking his cigarette into the ashtray, lifting his head once he noticed the door to the studio open. "Divine timing. Bob's back! Let's jam."

With his arms full, Bob held the door open with his foot, and smiled when he saw Jadon sitting there.

"Hey, dude, glad to have you back. Things don't feel right when you're gone. Not that you could help it. How's our Meg?" Bob asked, restocking the fridge with beer. "Can't wait to see her tomorrow. I hope we can drag her down here. Might lift her spirits."

"Or drag her down. Christ, she can't play right now," Stu grumbled.

"She's looking forward to seeing you guys. She's been feeling real anxious. I think she needs to be surrounded by everyone. I don't like to even leave her alone. Speaking of which, she's alone right now. Give me a quick run through of the song. Then I should get back," Jadon said.

Picking up his guitar, Chick knew it would take only a taste of the song before Jadon would write his own part in it. The riffs were hard played and felt with intensity. When Chick hit each chord it felt like he was drilling into the ground. And because of that, in many ways the guitar shaped the song. It was an anthem, a calling of arms. A song that echoed what Chick felt inside.

"Remember when we were first starting out, rehearsing in my garage up in that little house Erin and I had in Ventura? We recorded our first album in that garage. That's how I want to record this. I don't want it clean, I want it just like life, and life's sure as hell not clean," Chick said, grating his hand hard across the strings.

Jadon liked the way Chick instantly made the guitar hum, as if it were picking up momentum slowly but with power, magnetically pulling and picking up chords as he gained speed. Chick kept his chords direct, but made sure to coax the primal scream from each riff as he paused, letting the guitar cry out until its sound was dampened by Stu, who softened the intensity, and began creating the rhythm Jadon knew he would be falling in line with. Jadon felt his pulse quicken. Taking two long strides, he slid himself behind his drums. Chick turned and looked at Jadon and smiled, giving him the chance to catch up with the rest of them.

Jadon played within the chords as Chick worked through the song and back around, giving him ample time to find his own way. Jadon held silent during the pause, knowing Chick wanted to focus on the intensity of the scream his guitar was sending out, before joining with Stu with a quickened thump that made the body want to stand up and march toward the finish line.

Knowing Jadon had enough mapped out to keep steady with the rest of them, Chick leaned in to his mic.

Digging deep within himself, he howled out the words he knew he owned. The song and each word he wrote were meant to be yelled. This was his primal scream, his call to arms.

You're holding all the cards — game's always been yours
Been sitting across from you all night — at times I forget what for
Despite how it's been going — I can't throw my hand down
You know I'm tired from holding on — too tired to make a sound
What kind of game am I playin' if I'll never win?
The dreams laid out — but when will they begin?
I look around the table — the regular players all here
I'm done with the chase — I got nothing left to fear
Questioning the move I'll make — everyone's just staring at me
You go by the name God — then why do you feel like the enemy?
Looking at the door — I turn back around
Not afraid to go eye to eye — I demand one more round
Got to make it work — can't give in

The game's not over — this soul's made to win
Throw it at me — cuz I don't care where I've been
All I see is where I'm going — I'm ready to begin
It's not over yet — there's still cards left to play
This soul's not dead — I'm good for another day
This soul's made to win
This soul's made to win

Chapter 8

"When I ran to the studio yesterday, I sure as hell never thought my dad would show up while I was gone. Christ," Jadon said, tapping his fingers on the counter, staring at the toaster.

Placing small bottles of jam and honey on the tray, Meg slowly gathered as many things as she could find to create a one-handed, finger-friendly breakfast platter.

"He has to be at least six-four or more, and I have to say, he sure was interesting," she said, still feeling the effects of Jadon's father's visit.

"I bet. And he didn't say anything to upset you, or make you feel uncomfortable, did he?" Jadon questioned again.

Jadon had barely slept through the night, thinking of how Meg must have felt opening the door to find his father standing in front of her. Especially after all he had just shared with her. Pushing down the toast in the toaster for the second time, Jadon spun around and tightened Meg's robe again. So far she hadn't mastered tying a snug knot with one hand.

"Everything he did say was very poignant. Direct. And, well . . . ," Meg paused.

"I knew it. I knew there was something he said, that you hadn't told me about yet."

"It's not bad. I just didn't want to bring up *his* name last night. I liked listening to you tell me about the guys and the new song. I miss them. I miss being able to be *with* them. Not just a dope that stands around, but playing with them." Meg stopped to look toward the ocean and gather her thoughts. "From the moment I first played with you guys, it was like someone put an oxygen mask on me. I could breathe."

"You'll breathe again. I know it. You just don't know it yet. Now, please tell me what he said. It's ripping me up."

"Oh. Right. It was just odd. He asked if I'd heard from Devon," Meg said with a look of bewilderment.

Jadon's head shot back, surprised and startled to hear Devon's name. "Why the hell . . ."

"Yeah, I know. That's what I thought too. Then to add to it, I could tell he was really thinking about Devon. I felt like I'd been called in for questioning. Not that he felt I was guilty, more like he knew I was a key witness. Then later . . ."

"There's more?" Jadon said, taking the tray out to the balcony and setting it on the small table that faced the ocean.

"Yeah, he said . . . Devon is like a house on fire," she said, staring at her toast.

Jadon watched as Meg continued to look at her breakfast. He watched as she picked up the knife and stabbed the butter.

"Well, that's not going to work. That's not going to work at all." Meg put the knife down.

"Let me do it." Jadon sprung up to help Meg.

"I don't want you to butter my toast. I want to do it."

"You will. I want to get your mind off of what you can't do, and on to what you can." Jadon pointed to the jam.

"No, honey, please. I can't even drive. My car, yours . . . both stick shifts. I can't sign my name. I can't open a fucking bottle of water unless I squeeze it between my knees. Then once I get the cap unscrewed water pours out and all over the place . . . "

Jadon put his finger over Meg's mouth and said, "But you will. We're going to be sitting right here, not too long from now, and you'll be putting honey on my toast. Just because you want to show off."

Meg laughed. "I hope so. I want you to be so right about this."

"I am," he said, holding the spoonful of honey.

He touched her lip with the spoon. Meg grinned and opened her mouth. Tipping the spoon, Jadon let the honey pour slowly onto Meg's tongue and lower lip. Before she had a chance to close her mouth, he leaned forward quickly and pressed his mouth onto hers. Licking the honey from her lip, he opened her mouth with his, and licked the last remaining drop from her tongue.

With his eyes closed, he licked his lip and said, "Oh . . . oh, that was good."

"That was. Maybe this . . . situation does have its perks." Meg grinned.

Dipping the spoon back into the jar, Jadon placed it over Meg's mouth. She closed her eyes and tipped her head back. Carefully, he let the honey drop into her open mouth and onto her tongue. Once enough droplets had formed, he pressed his lips onto hers.

≈

"Think he'll keep it on?" Bob wondered, watching Chick wrap the big red bow around Larry's thick, white neck.

"Should. He seems to let you do pretty much anything to him. God, can't imagine why anyone would give up a dog like this." Chick shook his head in wonder.

"Maybe they had to. I have a feeling his owners didn't want to part with him," Flora said, rubbing her hand along Larry's back. "He feels very soft and clean."

"That's because we just picked him up from the beauty parlor," Stu said, lighting another cigarette. "He smells like flowers."

"He wasn't supposed to smell like a girl. I told them to use something masculine. I don't think they listened," Chick said, putting another piece of gum in his mouth.

Everyone felt tense. Excited to see Meg, yet tense about how she would receive Larry. Jadon was certain Larry would help Meg regain the use of her right hand. He felt it would distract her enough so that her subconscious would kick in. Or maybe it was the other way around; he wasn't sure. What he was sure of, though, was if Meg could just allow herself the chance, she'd begin using her hand.

Walking up behind Erin, Flora ran her hand across Erin's back. "Are you going to be sharing anything with us this evening?"

Erin nodded with a hesitant grin. "We want to. We can't wait. Depends how it goes though. This night belongs to Meg."

"Load 'em up," Chick said, motioning everyone out the door of the studio. "Come on, Larry, time to shine."

⁓

Jadon glanced around the kitchen, pleased with himself and the feast he managed to put together. Looking out the kitchen window, he stared at his beach house next door and thought about what Meg had said, which was confirmed when he talked with his dad earlier that morning. *Why does he need to stay in town longer?* Jadon wondered. He knew that his father's answer wasn't really an answer at all. Instead, all John had said was that he felt certain there are a couple matters needing his attention.

"I'll get it!" Meg yelled, hearing the doorbell.

Scooting past the sofa, Meg glanced at Jadon and gave him a warm smile. She felt good. Her family was near, she could feel it. Swinging the door open, Meg looked down and felt her heart melt.

"Well . . . who are you?" she asked, looking at the big white boxer sitting patiently at her door with his red bow still wrapped around his neck. Kneeling down, Meg stared at the large, square head that held an expression of non deliberate dissatisfaction. Sliding the envelope out from under his paw, she opened it. In a soft whisper, Meg read the handwritten note.

I hope you can help me. I've been chosen for you. I was left at the animal shelter and I need a new family. I was told, by a very reliable source, that you are an excellent Mother. When you are blue, I will cheer you. When you feel alone, I will sit next to you. When you are scared, I will protect you. I will love you until my heart draws its final beat.

~ Larry

Holding the note against her heart, Meg wiped the tears from her eyes, knelt and pulled Larry close.

"Looks like you've got a new home, Larry," she whispered into his ear.

"Yea!" Stu bellowed as he, Flora, Kofi, Chick, Erin and Bob hurried out from where they were hiding beside the house. "Good job, Larry. We told ya she'd love you."

"Come on in. Oh, good. Everyone's here. Finally," Meg said, letting everyone parade into her home behind Larry, who strolled in as if he knew the place well.

Flora wrapped her arms around Meg. Cupping Meg's face in her hands, Flora smiled and searched Meg's face. "You look good. How are you?"

"Good. I mean . . . ," Meg tilted her head with question.

Without doubt, Meg was a confusing mixture of good and bad. Often she didn't know which direction her emotions were heading until they got there, and usually they surprised her by how intensely they landed once they arrived at their destination.

Jadon quickly handed everyone a drink and ushered them into the living room.

Sliding next to Meg and Larry on the sofa, Stu offered into Meg's ear in a hushed tone, "Larry was Jadon's idea."

"Yeah, wish we could take the credit, but . . . he had us working on Larry for a while now," Chick smiled.

Meg looked at Jadon and tried to hold back her tears, unable to do so, she simply whispered, "Thank you."

"Aw, it's all right," Stu said, handing her a tissue.

"Yeah, Meggie . . .," Bob smiled, "you needed a furry dude around. And Jadon isn't exactly furry, except for that scrappy beard."

"God, just when I think you guys can't get any better, you do. You get better," Meg said.

Looking up, Meg caught eyes with Erin, sensing immediately Erin's anxious energy.

"How's therapy going, Meg?" Kofi asked, taking a swig of his beer.

"What has Dr. Solomon told you about where you stand with all this?" Flora added.

"Ha . . . they can't find any reason why I'm not getting mobility yet. It's probably me, I guess. Although they are still doing more tests. There is a list of restrictions . . . Quite a list of things I can't do. Enough to last a lifetime . . ." Meg stopped herself, remembering the look on Dr. Solomon's face during their last visit.

Looking up, Jadon saw Meg struggling with what Dr. Solomon had said. Jadon slid Larry to the side, and himself closer to Meg and ran his hand through her hair, brushing it away from her face.

"It's all right. There's a lot we don't know for sure. Those were just cautionary guidelines," Jadon said, trying to make gentle eye contact with Meg.

Shaking her head, Meg felt angry. "I have so much coming up. So much that I was so excited about. I finally found the courage to publish this last book under my own name; no longer hiding behind my tightly held anonymity. But I can't even manage a book signing. I can't sign my name. It's like, not only am I restricted, and having to relearn everything, but . . . the doctor analyzes one's future and starts checking things off. Can't do this, Meg, can't do that. *The type of stroke you had, at your age . . . it leaves you open for more strokes.*" Meg mimicked the words spoken by the doctor as she looked down. Closing her eyes she pinched off another wave of full flowing tears. "Can't run a marathon.

Okay, that's easy. I hate to exercise. Can't mess with illegal drugs. Easy as pie, don't want to touch them. Check. The list goes on and on until . . . you really shouldn't have a child. The damage is so extensive, you most likely won't be able to conceive, and if you do . . . they say so matter of fact, your chances of having another stroke might prevent you from even being able to go full term. Oh. Okay. No biggie. Check, check, and check."

Erin looked at Chick, then down at the floor. Flora wrapped her hand around Erin's and then extended her hand to Meg's. Gripping her fingers tight around Meg's, Flora shared her tears.

"It's okay, I guess. I don't think I'd be a good mom. But Jadon would make a wonderful, absolutely wonderful, father. And I can't give him the chance to find out."

"Well, that's fucked up. Christ. Like the stroke wasn't enough," Stu said, looking at Jadon then back at Meg. "Maybe they're wrong."

Jadon kissed Meg's ear. Looking around the room he took in the distraught faces. That was the most Meg had talked about what Dr. Solomon had said. Until now, she hadn't been able to even discuss it. Not that it needed to be discussed. He just wanted a life with Meg. He didn't need anything more than that.

"I know you'd be a great mom, Meg," Flora said, wiping her hands across her cheeks to clear her face of tears.

Erin pulled her arms tightly around her chest. "Maybe the prognosis will change as you heal," she said, hoping beyond belief she was right.

"Enough about me," Meg said, sitting up straighter. "I want to know about you. Each and every one. Keep me up till the wee hours. In fact, stay here for the night. I don't want you guys to go," she smiled, holding Jadon's hand tight within her own.

"Chickie here just wrote a kick ass song," Stu said, pointing his cigarette in Chick's direction.

"That's what a little bird told me," Meg said. "When do I get to hear it?"

"Well, we weren't sure how soon you'd be in the mood to come to the studio, but . . . man, we want you there. As soon as you're ready. It's waiting for you. It's real important you hear it, too. Real important," Chick said, propping his elbows on his knees while he sat next to Erin.

"How about now," Meg said, looking at Jadon. "Or after dinner, I mean."

"Cool with me. I *want* you to want to go the studio. We don't even have to eat dinner. The dinner I spent all day making," Jadon teased, winking at Meg.

"I'm stoked. I feel it. I feel it. The band's still solid. I'm fuckin' stoked," Stu said, smacking his hands together and giving them a quick mischievous rub.

Jumping up, Stu strutted to music only he heard as he made his way into the kitchen and grabbed a plate.

"Whatcha' got for us, Jay? What the hell are these?" Stu said, holding up a round, brown ball that he quickly threw into his mouth. "Whatever they are, they're good. Don't tell me what's in them."

"Falafel balls. They're for Flora and Kofi," Jadon said.

"There's no way in hell you made these little balls yourself?" Stu said, carefully studying another before putting it into his mouth.

"Whole Foods. That's where I got everything. Except the beer," Jadon said, getting up to make Meg a plate.

Finding an open space next to Meg, Flora took a seat and wrapped her arm around her. Swaying her body rhythmically back and forth, she began to hum.

"Am I going to beat this?" Meg asked sadly.

"I believe so. I know so," Flora answered, continuing her sway that included Meg and Larry, who quickly took Jadon's place next to Meg once the space became available again.

"How do you know? Because I don't know. Jadon says he does. But I think he's just telling me what he wants to have happen," Meg said quietly.

"I know, because I see it. Jadon knows it because his instincts are telling him to see only that which he wants, and by doing so he's setting the wheels in motion moving toward creating that end. The question is, sweetie, what you are creating," Flora said, giving Meg a kiss on the head.

Stepping into the studio, Meg took a deep breath. It felt like it had been forever since she last stepped foot into the place that started it all.

"Get you a beer, Meg?" Bob asked, opening the fridge.

"Sure. Yeah. Lay it on me. I am dying to hear this song," she said.

"Oh, you won't be disappointed. It smokes. We fuckin' burrow through the ground, then in the next riff Chick's shooting off like a rocket," Stu said, opening the door to the rehearsal room.

Chick walked to his guitar with a smile on his face. He liked to hear what was being said about the new song. Others were describing it exactly as it felt to Chick when he wrote it. Like throwing clay, he let the song write itself as he kept building onto it. Adding more instruments, more emotions, he kept letting it spin to life. Now, he was pleased with the creation.

Meg took a seat next to Erin, Flora and Kofi while the band took their places in front of them. Looking at Jadon, Meg smiled, noticing the glow resting comfortably on his face. He was at home again sitting behind his drums. She watched as his long blonde hair shrouded his face as he bent forward to pick up his sticks and adjust his stool. She kept her eyes cemented on him, taking in every moment, every movement. In doing so she felt a magnetic wave wash over her. Everything about him pulled at her heart and body, nudging her toward him. It was that way from the moment she first saw him.

Running his hand through his hair, Jadon tilted his head back to stretch his neck. As his head lowered, his gaze met Meg's. Her large eyes embodied everything he wanted to explore in the world, every feeling he wanted to express, every desire he wanted to fulfill. *Thank you, God,* he said to himself.

"Okay," Chick said, looking at Meg. "First of all, I wrote this after coming back from the hospital, after your stroke. You were still unconscious. Jadon was a mess. And something just kept fighting to get out of me. I sat and watched the sunset and I swear God talked to me. Hell if I know what he said. But he was talking. I don't know, maybe this song was what he said." Chick threw his hand hard across the strings of the guitar.

Meg sat and listened, watching the band do what they do best. Listening to the words, she had to grin. It was Chick. Through and through, it was his direct way of saying what needs to be said, telling the truth of souls who are seeking something more. The soul itself is designed to search. To not do so would be death, and yet death circles patiently within the search, waiting: waiting for the moment when the cards are thrown down.

Erin put her arm around Meg and beamed. Her face glowed with pride. Chick was a musical genius, and she knew it. Meg turned to watch Erin watch Chick, noticing that Erin's eyes were as bright as those of a child's watching Santa, full of hope and excitement.

The band silenced their instruments, except for Chick, who brought the song back to the heavy riff that started it. Instead of ending in abrupt silence, Chick kept the riff humming until it faded. In doing so he created the feeling that the song lives on even though it had ended. Long after Chick hit his last chord, Meg had the distinct sensation that the song was still playing.

"Wonderful!" Flora and Kofi yelled.

Erin nodded her head with approval. "That came together perfectly."

Without thinking, Meg tried to clap. Not able to, she threw her fist in the air and shouted with everyone else. She noticed the band was holding their positions as if waiting. Chick put his guitar down, spun around and grabbed the tambourine.

Handing it to Meg, Chick said, "Don't look at me like that. Just take it. I wrote this specifically with this in mind. I need you to play it. I need a low, repetitive snaky rattle. Keep it light, but steady. Follow Jadon's beat with it. Fall into place with him. You'll feel it when he gives the drums that flip up that keeps repeating itself. I need you to do that too, but keep it low and steady. Now take your spot, Goddamn it," he said, giving Meg a grin that showed every tooth.

Chick turned around and pointed to the stool to his left, near Jadon. Meg didn't move. She looked at Jadon, who motioned with his head to join them. Meg hadn't expected any of this. She felt awkward, knowing everyone would be watching not the hand that shook the tambourine but the one that remained motionless on her lap.

"Duty calls, your band is waiting," Kofi said, leaning around Flora to get a better view of Meg.

"Get up there. They get goofy now when you're not up there with them," Erin teased.

Standing up, Meg let out a deep sigh. She couldn't tell if Chick was just trying to find a way to make her feel like a part of the band again, despite the fact that it simply wasn't possible, or if he had actually wanted and intended for the tambourine to be part of the song, when he wrote it. It was obvious that Jadon, Chick, Stu and Bob weren't going to budge from their places until she did exactly as instructed.

"If this is a pity part, I'll know," Meg said, sliding up onto her stool, and giving Jadon a questioning look.

"Trust us," Jadon said, giving her a grin and quick thump and drum roll that made her laugh.

God, he's gorgeous, she chuckled to herself as she resigned to their wishes.

"I do. I trust you. All of you. I just don't want pity," Meg said, looking at Chick.

"It's not pity. This is the sound I heard when I saw the sun refuse to set that night," Chick said, beginning the song.

Within a moment of being within the song, Meg knew it wasn't pity. The sound fit. The song was a living, breathing person declaring its place in the world. And Meg loved it. More than anything, she loved being a part of it. It was the song she needed to hear, precisely when she needed to hear it.

There was no escaping the drums; they provided the heartbeat that sat in the background, yet powered the person. Stu and Bob offered the breath that moved instinctually in and out, slowing down only long enough to give the oxygen needed to fuel Chick, who blazed into a flurry of expression. He was the torch. His guitar provided the hand that angrily shoved its fist into the air, and pushed at whatever was in its way. His voice only mimicked what the guitar was able to say without words. And the low hum that Meg imbued into the song gave it eyes. While the voice screamed angrily, the eyes held unyielding onto their target.

Sitting with the band, surrounded by her family, Meg didn't care if she ever wrote one more word. She only wanted to be a part of the sound they were able to make together. Like a good novel, the music transported the mind and soul to places it wasn't able to go otherwise. Each song was a novel, accomplishing the same goal, only in a shorter amount of time. And being a part of Equinox made Meg feel stronger about her upcoming book tour. Maybe it was the song, maybe it was knowing she had a family that had her back if she failed; either way, sitting there, the only words streaming across Meg's mind were, *Fuck it. I'll do my best. No more, no less.* And those were the only words she needed.

Chapter 9

"Good afternoon," Arianna stated, with an expressionless stare directed at Meg.

"Good afternoon," Meg said, motioning for her to come inside.

"So this is the illustrious Area 51 Studio," Arianna said, giving the lounge a quick glance as she placed her briefcase on the coffee table in front of the sofa.

"Not sure how famous it is, but this is it."

Sitting across from her new assistant, Meg took advantage of Arianna's preoccupation with her papers and the upcoming itinerary to get a close look at her.

Arianna's slender frame was draped in a perfectly tailored black cashmere suit. Her skirt was at a faultless length that showed her well-toned legs without crossing the line of professionalism. Her black hair was cut pixie short, allowing full exposure of her youthful face. It was within that youthful face that Meg felt the need to hold her right arm closer to her chest. She couldn't help but notice her insecurities bubbling under the surface of her forty-year-old body. Meg felt confident with her looks; yet staring at Arianna, Meg felt all too well the decade or more that separated the two of them.

The fine lines around Meg's eyes showed her age like the first few, white whiskers that dust the chin of a black lab. In contrast, Arianna didn't have any lines, only a firm, bright, unemotional face. Sitting back in her chair, Meg wondered if a person's soul was revealed by the expression their face naturally held. If so, Meg concluded, Arianna didn't have a soul. And if she did, it was void of feeling. Then it hit her: Arianna's face resembled that of a model in *Vogue* magazine. Regardless of whether the models were or weren't happy, they all had the same expressionless stare — the exact same stare Arianna was currently giving Meg.

"Did you say something?" Meg asked, leaning forward.

"I did. I asked how you were feeling," Arianna repeated, letting her eyes get distracted by her BlackBerry.

"Good. I'm good. Hope you didn't mind meeting here. The band wants to meet you." Meg smiled once again, trying without success to pry a smile onto Arianna's face.

"I don't mind." Arianna slid Meg's itinerary across the table. "All right, let's begin. Handle House has added a few more appearances. It seems things have picked up momentum now that everyone has caught wind that Meg Scott is really the long awaited for Kathleen Kelly. Do you feel you will need any voice training?"

"Uh . . . ," Meg stammered. "No."

"If so, we need to get that started immediately. Did you set up the Facebook page yet, and the Twitter account?"

"No. No, I haven't. Maybe tonight . . ."

"Handle House is counting on you to give them 110 percent. That might mean music takes a backseat while you promote your book. As I am sure you knew when you signed on with Handle House, they are a boutique publisher," Arianna said, crossing her legs.

"Actually, they came recommended, so I didn't research them. I just trusted and relied on the fact that they were referred to me," Meg interrupted, feeling more than a little uncomfortable.

"You have two things going against you as far as Handle House is concerned. First, you are used to writing under an assumed name. You've developed a long career as a best selling novelist, yet you've never promoted even one single book. And all the efforts needed to keep your books in the spotlight were carefully handled by your previous publishing company. Now, much of this will fall on you, directly. You might very well feel overwhelmed, especially as you are not just Meg Scott. To your followers, they are finally able to meet and know Kathleen Kelly. Second, you are doing all of this on the heels of recovery. Handle House has sent me, but they are not the type of company that offers some of the advantages of a large publishing house."

Arianna finally stopped to take a breath. "But we will do our best. I will be with you at all of your engagements. With your diligence and undivided commitment, Handle House should be content and your contract not threatened."

"Why would my . . . ," Meg began.

"Hey," Jadon said, walking into the lounge with the band following behind.

"Oh. Arianna, this is Jadon and Chick. Stu and Bob. That's Larry . . . our dog. Erin and Flora had hoped to be here too, but they haven't gotten back yet." Meg looked toward the door.

"I'm actually on my way out," Arianna said, standing up and looking directly at Meg before she nodded her head at the band. "I will call later. Let me know when you are set with Twitter and on Facebook. Handle House wants to be able to add those links to your press material."

Arianna snapped shut her briefcase and walked to the door. Not turning around to offer a final gesture of farewell, she left the studio. As the door closed behind her, she took with her every drop of air left in the room.

"Was it me or was she not very friendly?" Bob asked.

"Something about her. Maybe it's just that she's so professional, but . . ." Chick said, pulling a cigarette from his pocket. "Sometimes professional crosses the line and becomes rude. I'm pretty sure she jumped over that line a long, long time ago."

Sitting across from Meg, Jadon looked at her for a second before saying anything. "What matters is what *you* think."

"She didn't exactly fill me with warm fuzzies, if that's what you mean. But I guess I don't need a friend. I just need someone to keep me on track. She was a bit overwhelming, though. She really drilled into my head how different it will be working with a boutique publishing company versus a larger one," Meg said, rubbing Larry's head.

"Boutique?" Stu said.

"I sort of thought a smaller publishing company would be more personable. Crazy as it sounds when I signed on with them, they were. Now this," Meg said, trying to ignore her uneasiness.

"She kinda reminded me of a fairy," Stu said, looking first up and then back down as he gathered his thoughts. "She doesn't seem as harsh when you think she's a fairy. It was the hair. That little fairy hair cut. It's hot, but not. All at the same time. Hot on a girl that smiles, I guess. She was kinda like . . . a mean fairy."

"Ready, Freddie? Let's hammer out some frustrations," Chick said, holding out his hand for Meg to join them in the rehearsal room.

⁓

Sitting in her rental car, Arianna waited patiently for Devon to answer his cell phone.

"Yes?" he said.

"I just met with her," Arianna said, opening her window only enough for her cigarette smoke to snake itself out.

"And?"

"And it went well. I think she is sufficiently overwhelmed. Exactly as you wanted," Arianna answered, starting the car when she noticed a white Jeep pull up alongside her.

"I need to know what she said."

"She mainly listened. She didn't seem happy. Until she introduced me to everyone."

"You're at the studio, I take it."

"Yes. She said the band wanted to meet me. I met her dog as well," Arianna said, backing out and onto the alley bordering the studio.

"Very good," Devon said, ending the call after Arianna offered every comment possible that gave him a clear portrait of her first meeting with Meg.

Tapping his cell lightly on his chin, he visualized the meeting Arianna just had. He constructed in his mind how Meg looked, how her words sounded . . . her tone and the way she said them. Looking at Meg's itinerary, he knew exactly the moment he would make his appearance and why.

Sitting on the beach next to Larry, John thought over the details his two phone calls had provided him.

Devon Hathaway was in New York City and had cancelled many of his scheduled engagements in London to be there. Although there were no visible lines connecting the dots, John felt certain, given enough time, Devon would be drawing a line with permanent ink that connected him with Meg.

As it was only a hunch, John didn't feel comfortable offering his thoughts to anyone. Decades as a detective had taught him well. Keep speculation silent, but on the tip of your tongue. John considered flying to New York. But there would be nothing gained by staking out Devon. Most of what he needed to learn regarding his whereabouts could be found using his connections in the force.

Looking down at Larry, John tried to walk the fine line that separates thinking a problem to the point of smothering the answer, and releasing the problem so the solution feels free to show itself all on its own.

"He's got someone here, working for him," John sighed. "If I'm right, he's got someone either circling Meg or already in place gathering information."

Devon, didn't have a criminal record. There were no red flags to alarm anyone. But John couldn't shake what he felt when his arm brushed against Devon's weeks ago. During his third attempt to visit Meg's hospital room to see Jadon, shortly after Meg had been admitted after the camping accident, John remembered vividly the tall, stately man who walked briskly past him. Although his long strides were hurried, it was the look in his eye that made John stop and turn around.

As Devon walked past him that day, John felt a wave of emotion. Staring at Devon as he waited for the elevator door to open, John casually walked back in his direction. Accompanying him on the elevator, John kept silent; not knowing who he was, only that something wasn't right. It wasn't until John was standing on the curb outside the hospital that he heard Meg's name.

John made a direct effort not to look in Devon's direction while he patiently listened as Devon updated the person on the other end of the cell phone of Meg's condition. As the conversation grew heated, John heard the name Hathaway Publishing. It was enough to go on: a face and two names, one of which belonged to the person his son was currently glued to inside the hospital. By the end of the night, John knew exactly who had brushed up against him, and his gut told him why the wave that crashed against him thundered with emotion.

It took more reading of online publicity and gossip articles than he cared for, and a few more phone calls oversees than he wanted, but within days he felt convinced his gut was right. Devon Hathaway was a house on fire.

John always did find it sickly ironic that people amused themselves by watching in theaters and on television the crimes and cruelty he was employed to protect them from. Hate and desire gave momentum to a movie. But John saw only the real-life end result, when hate and desire eventually burn the house down, and usually taking with them as many innocent bystanders as they could find.

John may have lost Emily, but before joining her, he knew he needed to shield Jadon from the flames he felt certain were coming his son's way.

Chapter 10

"Feels like it's been a long time since we first sat at this cafe," Meg said, looking across the busy street that freely allowed entertainment and visual preoccupation for the hungry patrons of the small eatery.

"I love Cafe' Azure. I don't get here as much as I'd like, though," Erin smiled.

"I don't think I've ever been here," Flora added, turning to get a better look around.

Sitting quietly while she waited for her wine, Meg thought about the new song Chick wrote. Chick never ceased to amaze her. She smiled knowing it would be the next big hit for Equinox; it was already written in the stars. She could see it. And he was right; the low repetitive hiss he wanted from the tambourine gave the song an earthy quality. Like a snake on the hunt, moving along swiftly and resolute toward its target.

"So, do you think you're ready?" Erin asked, putting her hand on Meg's.

"For the first interview? No. I've been practicing signing my name with my left hand all week. There's been therapy, more meetings with Arianna, which I really don't care for, voice work, and next they want photos." Meg laughed unhappily.

"You would think they could pair you up with someone better than Arianna," Erin offered.

"She probably is the best. Who knows. But, wow, we don't mix well. It isn't that she is mean, it's just that she's devoid of any niceness."

"I'd like to meet her. I have so many things rolling around inside of me about all this. I see a few images, but not like I usually do," Flora said, thanking the waiter for her drink.

"We caught only a glimpse of her. She was sitting in her car talking to someone," Erin said. "I can't help it. I get this overwhelming feeling she isn't one of the good guys. I know she's from your publishing company, but . . ."

"I know. I'm really not enjoying any of this. Most likely because . . . ," Meg looked down at her arm. "They want me to stand in front of everyone and speak about my book. No one will be listening to me."

"Your book is flying up the bestseller list. I'm sure they want to hear the author talk about it," Flora said.

"No. Maybe if it were on the radio, just my voice. But, no, they'll all be watching my right hand and arm."

"Maybe not. I mean, sitting here, no one would know," Erin said kindly.

"It hangs low, from the shoulder down. It's heavy, so it hangs lower. It's like the rest of my body just wants to expel it. You know, like a bad tentacle or something. The body wants to drop the part that's injured so it might grow back another one," Meg said, taking a larger than normal sip of her wine.

"I don't think you're shoulder hangs down that much more than on the left," Flora said, sitting across from her.

"Anyway, I'm like a walking, talking crime scene. Everyone loves a good accident. There's this primal urge, even though they wince slightly, they still strain their necks to see the carnage."

"How is therapy going?" Erin asked.

"Okay. Well, depends . . . not a lot happens. But it's not like a meeting with Arianna, either," Meg chuckled. "I want to hear about you two. I miss you both. They've had me busy trying to prepare for these book signings, which are a joke, and the interviews. When all I want to do is wrap my arms . . . ," she paused, "or at least one arm, around Jadon, and be at the studio with everyone."

"All right, let's just girl talk it," Flora offered, lifting her glass.

"I like that. Let's girl talk it," Meg said.

Meg let her soul get nourished by friendship amply supplied by Flora and Erin. Laughing at the shared stories, and feeling their warmth as it encircled her, helped to wash away the residue of her limitations.

"If your yoga classes get any bigger, people in the back row won't be able to see you," Erin laughed, looking at Flora.

"I know. I might have to split my early morning class into two. I felt certain my unhappiness as of late would interfere with my teaching, but it seems just the opposite has occurred," Flora said, staring across the street.

"People feel your intensity. They feel that you aren't a demigod who doesn't walk in this world. Instead you're raw, and you're reaching to feel better, just like they are. They feel that," Meg said. "The best teachers are the one's that have walked the walk. People can relate better. When people relate, their guard goes down. That's my take on it anyway."

"I think you're right," Flora nodded.

"Meg," Erin said, "I'm dying to know, as is Flora even though she's too mature to bring it up: how's it going now that you and our beloved Jadon are living together? You two are together almost constantly. We watched you two for months longing to be with one another, so . . ."

"Ha. Well . . . *real* nice," Meg said, letting out a delicious laugh. "Real nice."

Erin beamed, looking at Flora, then back at Meg, "Details. Unfiltered details please."

"He sort of blows my mind, he is so passionate," Meg said, leaning in toward the table. "It's like..." She paused to look at the buildings across the street. "It's like my body has found its perfect medicine. Medicine that heals all the damage, all the hurt and disappointment. It's divine and delicious at the same time. He did this thing with honey the other morning . . ."

"Honey?" Flora smiled, "Nutritious *and* delicious."

"I knew it. I just knew it. From the moment I watched him sing and play that song he wrote for you." Erin grinned, taking a drink of her cucumber water

"Ha! I lose myself. In his eyes, his touch . . . I'm gone. I don't think of one other thing," Meg said, recalling their lovemaking from that morning.

"Are you going to incorporate any of that into a new book?" Erin asked.

Meg looked at Erin, then let her eyes linger on her face before answering. "I can't see how I would write. I don't want to even think about that right now. Fortunately, there aren't any voices wanting to get out and onto the page. Erin, you still haven't told me what the doctor said when you went for a visit last week. You're checkup went well, didn't it?"

Erin looked down at her glass, then at Flora.

"This is a good thing. Meg can handle it. I think she'd be happy to know," Flora said, rubbing her hand on Erin's back.

"I'm pregnant, Meg."

Chapter 11

Things were moving along exceptionally well, and Devon couldn't have been more pleased. According to Arianna and the many reports he'd read, Meg glowed like a seasoned professional during her first series of interviews. And Meg's book signing engagements went off without a hitch. Shortly after she opened the first book presented to her at Book Soup on the Sunset Strip in West Hollywood, and signed a well penned, left-handed *Meg,* Devon knew she wasn't about to fold anytime soon.

Regardless, Devon was pleased. The dates on the calendar were quickly unfurling and would soon provide him with the day in which he would be face to face with her again. He was ready, and by then, he knew, so would she.

Even though Meg was dealing well with the onslaught of public attention, Arianna was making certain Meg felt every pound of pressure that was carefully pressed upon her. Adding to the mix was the unexpected but welcomed legal setback that had arisen when a struggling author claimed Meg had copied his work.

Ridiculous, Devon thought, as the book was based on Meg's own mother. He smirked at the absurdity. But such was always the case within the publishing world, as well as the music industry. Coattail riders were always busy grasping on to the long, fluttering tails of talented artists. They were often misguided by the adage *any publicity is good publicity*. Unfortunately for them, their hope for it to be true didn't always make it so.

Devon was well acquainted with the many hurdles, obstacles and the otherwise unseemly side of the publishing world, the world he had protected Meg from ever since he published her first book. Now he allowed that world to dance obnoxiously around her; taunting and demanding from her with every turn.

By now a new assistant would have been sent in, dates would have been rearranged, and the Hathaway legal department would have tweezered out the ticks that tried to attach themselves to Meg. Devon didn't like that Meg had to feel the unpleasantness she was being made to feel. Yet, he took comfort knowing that soon he would make it all go away.

⁓

"What's wrong?" Jadon asked, watching Meg walk into the rehearsal room at the studio.

"Apparently, there is this man saying much of my novel was stolen from a piece of work he created years ago," Meg said, bewildered and confused as she sat down on the chair in front of Chick.

"What the fuck?" Chick questioned, snapping his gum. "That's flat out bullshit. Man, vultures are always flying around."

"Arianna said that Trish is looking into it. She also said that I have to fly to New York in a few days. They want me to appear at the book fair. I guess it's a big deal," Meg said, unhappy with the new information.

"Oh, man, when is that? It better not be on Friday. We have a gig we can't get out of," Chick said.

"Of course, it's on Friday," Meg sighed, looking at Jadon. "Don't worry. I'll be fine. I just wish you could be with me, though."

Jadon looked at Chick and leaned his head to one side waiting to hear that their show could be rescheduled.

"Sorry. The label won't budge. They've already sold the tickets. It's sold out. One-night show." Chick shook his head side to side slowly. Pulling his pack of Lucky Strikes from his pocket, he took a seat in front of Meg.

"Well, this stinks. So Meg can't be there?" Stu asked.

"What time do you have to appear at the book fair? The show doesn't start until ten o'clock our time," Chick said, with an instinctual finger point to the ground. His hope was that they might be able to use the time difference to their advantage. "As soon as you say your last word, we'll jet you back if we have to."

Sitting up in her seat, Meg's mind began to calculate with hope. "Well, my appearance is at one in the afternoon. I'm not sure what's required after that. But maybe . . ."

"Chick?" Jadon said, hoping there was a way Chick would be able to pull it together.

"Fuck it. We'll make it happen. I want to do the new song at the end of the show, so . . . yeah, we'll make this happen." Chick pulled out his cell phone and ran his finger across the screen. "Vince . . . we got a problem," he said, as soon as their manager picked up on the other end.

⁓

Pulling into Chick's driveway, nestled in the hills that bordered Bay City, Jadon turned and looked over at Meg. "You sure you're ready for this? It's been a freakishly long couple of days on top of one hell of a long day of shopping for baby things."

"Yeah. Before I head to New York, I want Erin and Chick . . . to know how happy I am for them. And she said she didn't want a baby shower, so that means we'll just have to lavish an endless supply of gifts on them right up until the little critter makes its appearance," Meg smiled.

"You're really something, you know that?" Jadon said, cutting the engine. "God, I love you."

"I'm something, all right."

Walking into the house, Meg was able to carry only what her left arm would hold. Jadon was already on his second trip back from the car, with arms loaded heavy with boxes of all shapes and sizes.

"Oh, my God!" Erin screamed softly, still feeling overjoyed that Meg had arranged a gathering to celebrate her pregnancy. "I'm so excited."

"Good. You should be." Meg gave her a nudge.

"Whoa. We're goin' to be up till midnight opening up all these. Add them to the pile everyone else brought," Chick said, thrilled with the attention Erin was getting.

Both he and Erin couldn't ignore the cloud that unavoidably followed the news of Erin's pregnancy. Coming right on the cusp of learning Meg shouldn't and most likely couldn't ever have kids, made celebrating their own good fortune almost impossible. But it was obvious Meg saw the dark cloud and was doing all she could to allow the parade to continue - rain or shine.

"Erin, I don't think I've ever seen you look so radiant," Meg said, giving her a hug. "How do you feel?"

"Good, I feel good. Tired, but I don't mind," Erin said, tucking her long brown hair behind her ears.

Taking a seat next to Flora, Meg rested her body into hers, just as a child would think nothing of reclining into the warm body of their mother. In many ways that was how Meg felt with Flora. She wasn't just a pair of receptive arms; Flora exuded safe, healing energy. Whenever she was around, Meg tried to absorb as much of it as she could

As instructed, Chick captured as many moments as his camera would hold. Meg told him she wanted to compile the pictures into a photo album for Erin, with the hope that the many pages of the album would record and bear witness to the miracle growing inside of Erin.

Snapping his gum happily, Chick told Flora and Meg to squeeze together. "You two, tighten up, I want a good shot."

"Don't waste it on us!" Flora laughed.

"This memory card holds a gazillion pics, and I'm going to fill it up," Chick said, lowering himself in front of them for a close-up shot.

"Babe." Erin motioned for Chick to sit next to her. "I want to share our decision, and see what they think."

"Cool. Let's do it," Chick looked at everyone intently. Waiting for Erin to speak, Chick turned and looked at her: "You want me to . . . or you?"

"You," Erin said, taking a deep breath.

"Okay. Well, we've given this *a lot* of thought. And it's real important to us. Meg, Jadon . . . we'd like you to be this baby's godparents."

"You bet! Absolutely," Jadon said as he turned to look at Meg.

Meg stared at Erin. She felt not only honored, but overwhelmed and overjoyed, all of which cut off her ability to speak. Holding her hand to her mouth, she nodded, *yes*.

Like an entertainer taking his final bow to the audience before walking off stage, the sun dipped into the ocean, letting Meg know the day was coming to a close. Sitting with her toes dug deep into the sand, she turned once she saw Jadon and Larry jogging back from their trip down the beach. Throwing his body next to Meg, Jadon leaned over for a kiss.

"Miss me?" he said playfully.

"Did, and always will."

Pleased with her answer, Jadon watched the waves roll onto the shore. Once the darkness ushered out the day, the ocean put on its favorite nighttime performance; it was a performance that Meg, Jadon, and now Larry made a point to get first row seats to each and every night. Like acrobats dressed in white, the caps of the ocean waves tumbled wildly toward them. And just like true circus performers, the waves made it appear as if they weren't in control, all the while, every moment was choreographed and executed with precision.

"So . . . I know that hit you pretty hard earlier. Talk to me," Jadon whispered, keeping his eyes on the largest acrobats that stayed in the distance.

"Uh, oh . . . I couldn't be happier for them." Meg winced from the bitterness and joy she felt. "No one deserves it more," she said, resting her head on her arm as she looked at Jadon.

"You do," he said tenderly. "You do."

"It seems Fate feels differently."

"Fate's been good to us. Here we are. There were days, too many days, when I would sit and look out at this ocean and dream of having you in my life. Not just on the outskirts, not just in the band, but with me. Every morning, Meg, I wake up and thank God for you."

"I do the same, about you. I'm so confused. How is it, I would long for the day when I could wrap my arms around you, then to finally have you, and not be able to wrap my arms around you? Not completely anyway. Not as I had envisioned. But I look at you and . . . ah . . ."

Turning to face Meg directly, Jadon placed her right hand onto his.

"I was going to do this later, but . . . I don't like that you are going away without me. Even if for just a day. And I don't know what you'll think of it, with your feelings about this subject. But . . . ," Jadon said, leaning back to dig into the front pocket of his jeans. "I saw this stone, when we were in Oslo on tour last year. I thought it was so beautiful, just like you, so I bought it. I wasn't sure what to do with it. I wanted you to have it, to wear it as a . . . symbol of how I feel about you. So I threw caution to the wind and had it made into a ring. I want you to wear it, if you want."

Jadon handed Meg a small ring that cradled a large pink translucent stone. The delicate silver threads, encircling the stone, held it in place with thin strips that gently met on the sides to form the band. The detailed artistry of the ring held the glimmering pink stone in place with delicate ribbons of silver.

"It's a rose quartz. I was told at the shop where I bought it and the bracelet I gave you, that rose quartz is the universal stone of love. So . . . I want you to wear it knowing that wherever I am, wherever you are, I love you." Jadon kept his eyes on Meg's as she stared at the ring she held in her hand.

Handing it back to Jadon, Meg smiled, "I would be honored to wear it, only, though, if you put it on my finger."

Holding her left hand out, the only hand she could, Meg spread her fingers and waited for Jadon. Looking first into Meg's eyes, Jadon gave her a small kiss, then placed it on the finger he most hoped it would fit.

"Thank God, it fits," Jadon said, relieved. He would have been happy with whatever finger she had it on, as long as she wore it. But deep down, he wanted it on the finger it was now on.

In her left hand Meg held Jadon's face. Looking into his eyes, she silently thanked God for all that she'd been given in him. When she noticed the mischievous look slowly emerging on his face, she had to smile.

Giving Meg a kiss that slowly pushed her body onto the beach, Jadon slid his body on top of hers. As his long blonde hair created a curtain surrounding their faces, he brought his lips onto hers.

Chapter 12

Walking alone on the sidewalk outside Meg's house, Jadon waited patiently in the dark while Larry zigzagged in front of him. As was the normal routine, Larry was unable to decide which side of the sidewalk held a more fascinating scent.

"Meg home?" John asked, walking up behind his son.

Jadon spun around quickly. "Dad! Christ. You scared the hell out of me. It's fucking four a.m. What are you doing out here?"

"Is Meg home?" John repeated.

"No. She had to fly to New York this morning. She has an appearance at some book fair. She left just minutes ago. The band flew her out, so we have a jet on standby waiting for her to come back as soon as she's done. Why?"

John took a deep sigh. *This is the beginning,* he thought. Rubbing his finger across his bottom lip, he thought over the obvious discovery. Meg was alone, exactly as Devon would have hoped. It wasn't until moments ago that John learned from his friend at La Guardia Airport that the Hathaway jet was getting prepped for an evening flight to Los Angeles. *Why a flight out to the west coast, right on the heels of Meg landing in New York?* John asked himself.

"You watch Larry for me?" John asked, handing Jadon Larry's leash.

"Yeah. But why? Where are you going? Does this have to do with Meg? Dad. Damn it. What's going on?" Jadon yelled. "Is this about that whole *Devon's a house on fire* thing?"

Turning around, John looked at his son, his face resembling an emotionless statue that gave no indication of hope or tragedy. There was too much John was unsure of, but the one thing he knew for certain: Jadon needed to be in one piece, safe and secure to take care of Meg. It was obvious Meg needed him and what Jadon would give her. John didn't feel right not being completely honest. But he was going on a hunch and sometimes hunches are wrong — although his rarely were.

"I think someone needs to be watching over Meg, that's all," John said. "Trust me."

"What? You can't just say that and leave. Are you fucking serious? Is she all right? What aren't you telling me? Goddamn it. I better go to New York. I have to be with her. Christ." Jadon's voice and the look on his face revealed the waves of panic tumbling over his body.

"No. You be here for when she returns. I'll be back. I just have a feeling. I'm probably wrong. I just want to watch over some things," John said, trying to make an exit.

"You're fucking never wrong about these things!" Jadon shouted, noticing his words weren't stopping his father.

Jadon raked his fingers through his hair. Looking down at Larry and Larry, he grabbed his cell phone and flipped it open. His chest tight with fear, he waited for the other line to pick up.

"Chick. Something's going on. My dad is going to New York to watch over Meg. He won't tell me why other than he thinks someone should be with her. He knows something, and he's not telling me. I'm fucking freaking out and don't know what to do. He told me *not* to go, which makes me want to go even more. If she needs someone, I need to be there. Get here as fast as you can . . . Okay? Okay." Jadon rattled his words off so quickly the only word he heard from Chick was a final *okay* before he flipped his phone closed.

Jadon heard the sound of his dad's truck roar to a start, then back out of the driveway and roll smoothly onto the road heading in the direction of the airport.

~

"There are quite a few people here," Meg said, turning to watch the last few open seats in the large press room fill up.

"Is that going to be a problem?" Arianna said.

"Uh, no. No. Just making an observation," Meg said, looking at her phone.

Jadon sent me another text, and called again, Meg said to herself. Reading the text, she had to wonder what was up. General concern was sweet, but Jadon seemed downright worried, yet repeated adamantly that he wasn't.

MEG. R U OKAY?

Misses me already, does he? Meg smiled.

I'M FINE. MISSING YOU. GET ME OUT OF HERE :(

Meg hit send before trying to dial her voicemail. *No signal. Wonderful,* she mused. Looking around, she leaned over to ask Arianna if there was time to check her messages. To which Arianna simply shook her head, *no.* Taking a dissatisfied sigh, Meg listened as the announcer thanked everyone for joining them. Then he began to discuss the many books Meg penned under her assumed name. Cringing slightly, she had hoped the last book she wrote, the one about her mother, the one she wrote under her real name, would be the focus of the appearance; but she was wrong. After what seemed like an overly long introduction, the announcer kindly called Meg's name.

Walking across the stage and stepping behind the podium, Meg felt like a newly ordained preacher about to give their first sermon. Standing tall, she used her left hand to place her right hand on the edge of the podium; she hadn't wanted to wear the sling that had recently become her most worn fashion accessory. Instead she wanted only her words to captivate the audience, not her misfortunes.

"Hello. As you know, I'm Meg Scott. Thank you for joining me today. And thank you for the kind introduction. I take joy in discussing all of my novels, as each one was birthed by a new thought, a new vision. But the one I am most proud of is the one where I gave my mother wings to fly," Meg said, scanning the audience. "I think I'd like to start not with a well rehearsed speech, but with a discussion that stems from a question. So . . . ask *something*, and let's begin."

Noticing the sea of hands, Meg looked at Arianna for assistance. Quickly, Arianna walked to the front row and handed the young man with a press badge a microphone.

"Ms. Scott, this is a rare and long awaited pleasure. Please tell us where the inspiration for your latest book came from."

"Well. My mother," Meg laughed gently. "She was a wonderful woman, but her life was tragic. Not all of it, of course. Or as her daughter, at least I'd like to think it wasn't all tragic. But . . . for all that was good, there seemed to always be something bad. A sunny day, with too many storm clouds on the horizon. Or sometimes, oftentimes, storm clouds that shrouded the sun completely."

Meg looked down briefly. Regaining her focus, she ran her hand through her hair and pointed to another person, and again Arianna handed the microphone to someone from the press.

"Has Jadon's drug abuse affected your writing in any way?" The young woman asked, with an inquisitive tone.

"Uh. Pardon me?" Meg said.

"Well, you two seem to be close, and it is obvious the part of Jadon in *Love's End* was inspired by *your* Jadon. Or at least in looks, and perhaps a bit more. Yet the Jadon in *Love's End* never struggled with drugs," the young woman said, trying to be as exact as she could.

"Uh . . . ," Meg began to stammer. She never knew Jadon had any problems with drugs, and if he had she couldn't understand why it was being brought up now. "A novel, even one consisting of numerous pages, chapters and words, is still just a snapshot at best. Maybe Elle's Jadon has struggled with a few things, and if he has, surely it made him into the beautiful, raw person Elle fell in love with."

Devon marveled at Meg. He had secretly hoped she would've shown more signs of frustration from the last question. Instead she answered it not like a politician with words that twist and contort but like a poet, with words that stem from an eternal well of eloquence and truth. Folding his arms across his chest, Devon waited in the dark background while Arianna strategically gave the microphone to all the assigned people. In doing so, Devon believed their questions would have a cumulative effect, one that would, at some point, overwhelm Meg.

Devon listened as one interviewer after another asked questions ranging from the straightforward to the bizarre. He listened as Meg fielded questions about the man claiming that Meg stole his manuscript to ones having to do with her not being able to play the violin anymore. Devon was delighted when Equinox was brought into the fray: their lives, speculation concerning drug abuse, and whether she would ultimately retire from writing to pursue music.

"I . . . honestly don't know what any of this has to do with my novels. If you'd like to discuss those, I'd be more than happy to. But my friends, they are my family, and I would like to let them speak for themselves regarding anything they have or have not done," Meg said, showing signs of frustration.

Taking the microphone from Arianna's outstretched hand, the young man in tan slacks looked up at Meg and smiled. Glancing down at his notes he began, "Although you've known this for some time, we've only recently discovered that you lost your parents at a young age. How has this helped your writing career?" he asked with no sensitivity.

As if struck by lightning, Meg stood unmoving, burned in place, staring at the young man. Shaking her head, she couldn't believe the cruelty and callousness of the words he chose, and the heartless way with which he said them. Holding her fingers to her lips, Meg stood motionless while everyone looked on.

"Ms. Scott . . . ," he said, waiting for her response.

Nodding her head, Meg concluded that she'd had enough. She wasn't going to answer. Looking up, Meg offered only a mouth that did not frown but did not smile. Instead, much like her mother's had been for much of her life, Meg's expression was suspended somewhere in between. Letting her eyes scan the many faces looking back at her, Meg noticed the tall shadow of a man briskly making its way toward the stage.

Devon kept his eyes held softly on Meg's while her eyes were held in disbelief on his. Offering a compassionate smile, he stepped behind the microphone and cleared his throat quietly before beginning.

"I am amazed and astounded by what I've heard this afternoon," Devon said, taking the well rehearsed moment to let his presence silence the large crowd. "When an author steps before you to share their genius, they should be shown not only respect but kindness. Ms. Scott has been shown neither," he paused to glance at Meg. "It's true that Ms. Scott is no longer my client. But I consider her, and always will, my friend. I will not allow my friend to be treated in this manner. It takes courage to write, and it takes even more courage to discuss one's writing. I, for one, applaud Ms. Scott. Her private life is just that, private. You fell in love with her because of her writing; I recommend that you not forget that. And in closing, if *ever* Ms. Scott's friends or those closest to her are used for your fodder, either in print or at an appearance such as this, you will answer to me. I *will* have your press passes suspended if not revoked. You would do well not to forget that Hathaway Publishing is part of a much, much larger enterprise, one that spans not just that of the publishing industry, but of the music and film industry as well. I have a far reaching wing span. I leave you with that warning."

Devon stepped back from the podium and gave Meg his warm smile and bright eyes. Holding Meg's arm, he walked her down from the stage and out of the room.

"Are you staying in this hotel?" he asked with tenderness. "If so, I'll see to it you are taken back to your room so you may rest."

"Uh. No. I'm supposed to fly back as soon as this is over," Meg said, astonished by the sermon Devon just delivered.

"I wrote down the names of the imbeciles who harassed you. I will revoke their press passes. It's not right what they did. It wasn't fair to you, or to your friends. You have all been through too much already. Some . . ." He paused to look down at Meg's hands. "Some of which was from my own doing. When does your plane leave?"

"Not for a bit. Considering I was suppose to last a lot longer up on the stage. I don't know if I feel very good right now," Meg said, taking the nearest seat she could find.

"Do you need me to call anyone? Where is your help? Surely you have someone who helps you?"

"Arianna. But, no, don't get her. I don't want her . . . ," Meg said, wiping her hand over her face.

"All right. Do you need a nurse? Water? I can get you water," Devon said, looking around the lobby.

"You must have things to do. I don't mean to keep you."

"Oh, Meg. Well. Ah . . . ," Devon said catching himself, not able to share the words wanting to be said. Instead his mouth gave Meg a grin that easily and honestly revealed the love he felt. "It can wait. It can always wait where you're concerned."

Looking around the lobby, Devon saw the restaurant located off to the side. Although filled to capacity with patrons, he took Meg's hand and walked her inside.

"We're taking a table for two. And a bottle of Aqua Panna," Devon said to the host guarding the entryway.

Pulling a chair out for Meg, the host laid their menus on the white linen table, and motioned for the waiter to provide the water Devon requested.

"Are you all right? I'm not yet convinced. I feel I need to call someone. Or have *you* call someone. Are your friends here? Shall I get someone to find them?" Devon asked, keeping his palms together in front of his face while he watched Meg collect her senses.

Taking a long sip of water, Meg ran her hand behind her neck and waited for her mind to clear. Taking another long drink, she put her glass down with a sigh of defeat as she watched Arianna walk into the restaurant.

"Ms. Scott, we need to discuss how things went this afternoon. Although many of the questions were not polite, nor appropriate, Handle House does need you to do your best to fulfill the time requested of you," Arianna said, looking down at Meg.

Tilting her head to one side, Meg looked up at Arianna and couldn't believe what she was hearing.

"Ms. Foist is it?" Devon asked.

"Fiest," Arianna answered.

"My apologies, Ms. Fiest . . . your services are no longer needed. Ms. Scott will be finding another assistant of her own choosing. Thank you for your time," Devon said, motioning with his eyes toward the door.

Showing no emotion, Arianna looked at Meg, then back at Devon, before she turned slowly and walked out the door.

Leaning in toward Meg, Devon whispered, "I think you could do better placing an advert in your local newspaper. I hope you don't mind, but she was truly appalling. Perhaps I've overstepped?"

Meg shook her head, "No. I've been thinking of doing that myself. But Trish never gets back with me, and the appearances and obligations keep rolling in. I had hoped to just see it through and then be done with her."

"How are you, Meg? I've been worried," Devon asked, changing the subject.

"I don't know how I am." Meg rubbed her hand over her face again, unwittingly revealing once more the brilliant ring Jadon had given her.

"And the band?" Devon asked, looking from Meg's hand to her eyes.

"They're good. Devon . . ."

"Okay. I know. All right. Let's get back to the task at hand. Things are spiraling out of control. I've heard about the legal troubles you've been in. Silly, really."

"Yes, they are. It's almost too much for me to wrap my mind around," Meg sighed, feeling a bit more relaxed

"Would you like me to take care of him for you?"

"I would like him gone. But, I should let Trish handle it." Meg wished she could simply say yes.

"Meg, can you ever forgive me? No, don't say anything. Because what I did, to you, to your friends, is without forgiveness. I know that. I will have to live with that till my last day. I would like to say I am a changed man. I'm not. I am only changed in that I've learned you can't force someone to love you as you love them. I still want the same for you. I want for your happiness. That will never change. I would move heaven and earth for you Meg. I have the ability to do so. Perhaps you will allow me to help, even in the slightest, smallest way, just to show you that. To show your friends that as well. If I have lost my place within your world completely, I will accept that. I hurt you. I would sooner die than hurt you," Devon said, looking down at the table then softly toward Meg.

"I . . . I don't know what . . . to say." Meg tried to gather together some sort of logical reply.

"Talk it over with Jadon," Devon said, letting out a deflated chuckle. "Of course, I doubt he will allow me to help you. But perhaps he will understand that I can provide you the freedom to write, and to do so at your leisure . . . and to promote your books within a schedule shaped around you, one that allows you the ability to make music with Equinox, and travel with them. To do what you want to do. Permit me to do that. Discuss it with him if you'd like. I will text you later perhaps, ensuring that you are back home safe and sound. Let's get you in your car and back on your plane."

Standing up, Devon didn't want to give Meg the time to do anything except get safely on the plane. Walking her out of the hotel, and standing on the sidewalk, he looked down the street.

"My dear, do you have a car waiting? Perhaps you should take mine." Devon said, motioning to the limousine that was parked and waiting for him.

"I have to call for one. I wasn't sure when I would be done. Arianna was to call for one, actually." Meg laughed at the pitfalls of firing one's assistant so abruptly.

"Very well," Devon motioned for his driver. "Be well, Meg. I will be checking on you later," he said, helping Meg into his car once the driver opened the door.

~

Scanning the press room one last time, John pulled aside a reporter and asked where Meg Scott was. The reporter delighted in filling him in on the details that unfolded during her brief appearance. He explained how the line of questioning kept taking an almost calculated, personal turn, until eventually Meg was speechless. And how Mr. Hathaway had come to her aide, chastised everyone and had within minutes of leaving the room revoked the press passes of the interviewers who had asked inappropriate questions. From there the reporter didn't know where the two went, only that Mr. Hathaway had helped Ms. Scott out of the room and into the lobby.

Discouraged that he hadn't been able to get a flight out of LAX sooner, John turned toward the lobby and watched as Devon walked back into the hotel and down the long corridor leading to the elevator. Keeping his distance, John grabbed a flier from the conference and buried his face behind its pages, looking up only when he saw Arianna walk by and toward the same elevator. Walking casually behind her, John patiently waited with Devon and Arianna for the elevator doors to open. Stepping inside, John erred on the side of caution and pushed the floor just beneath the one chosen by Devon. John didn't ignore the fact that Arianna didn't push a button; apparently she would be stepping off the elevator with him or would be staying to step off on the top floor with Devon. Staring at the skyline through the glass walls of the elevator, John watched as the transparent box that held them scaled up the side of the building.

Looking at the formidable man standing next to him, Devon tried to remember where he had seen him before. Taking his cell phone from his coat pocket, he quickly dialed out and waited for the call to be answered.

"See to it there are no troubles. She needs to be on her jet and headed back to LA immediately. Then bring the car back. I'm leaving once you get here," Devon said in a crisp British cadence before sliding his phone back in his pocket while watching John exit the elevator.

Stepping off the elevator, John waited for the elevator doors to close behind him before pushing an UP button; almost instantly the doors to an adjacent elevator opened. John stepped in and punched the button for the top floor. A moment later, the doors opened, and John cautiously stepped out and in doing so was amused to see Devon leaning against the wall in front of him; his tall frame relaxed, his eyes scanning the screen of his cell phone. Walking past Devon, John kept his pace steady as he rounded the corner and walked down the hall.

Watching the familiar figure walk past him, Devon kept his face occupied with his messages, while his eyes carefully studied the large man who had just moments ago been on the same elevator with him. Shaking his head, Devon couldn't place the face. But there was no escaping it; he had looked into those eyes before.

Knowing there was a good chance Devon was on to him, John kept his distance. Sitting in the lobby, he slowly scanned the newspaper that was spread out across his crossed legs. He didn't move, even when he noticed Arianna walk out the doors of the lobby. And it took all the control he could find not to look up when he saw Devon within moments following behind her. Looking out the glass doors of the lobby, John watched as Arianna hailed a cab. He knew that if Meg hadn't planned on spending the night in New York, neither should have her assistant. Therefore there was no reason for Arianna to be visiting a hotel room, not to mention one on the same floor as Devon.

Noticing that Devon's footsteps stopped at the lobby doors, John looked up. He watched as Devon casually turned in his direction. With his hands relaxed in his trouser pockets, Devon stood tall and picturesque, staring at him. There were no signs of worry, or insecurity on Devon's face. Staring back, John made sure to show only the same.

～

Jadon flipped his phone shut, and flopped down between Larry and Larry on the sofa in the studio.

"Well, don't leave us hanging dude," Chick said, looking at Stu and Bob then back at Jadon.

"She said she's good. She didn't see my dad at all. There was a problem during the conference, though, but she made it to the jet in plenty of time. She's tired. She said she had to walk off the stage. She said she'd explain more once she got back to L.A. Christ . . ." Jadon looked at Chick. "She said Devon helped to get her back on time, and arranged for her to use his car. Fuck!" he said, tossing his phone on the table.

"What?" Stu groaned. "That motherfucker. He just couldn't wait. Goddamn it."

"He's one sneaky son of a bitch," Chick said, beginning to pace. "But she's on the plane and heading home, right?"

"Yeah. This isn't good. This is not good," Jadon repeated

"She didn't see your dad, though?" Bob asked

"No. She seemed kind of surprised I was asking. She said that Devon fired Arianna. Now she has to find a new assistant, but she is glad to be done with Arianna once and for all. I guess these asshole reporters were bringing up a bunch of shit about each of us. Especially me. Finally they brought up her parents' accident and she froze. That's when Devon stepped in. He fucking swooped right in. It's like he's God or something," Jadon said, throwing his hands over his face.

"Obviously we're going to have a little talk with your dad. He knows something," Chick said nervously.

"And here we sit. Trapped," Jadon said, talking into his hands.

"But Meggie's coming home. Let's just meet her at the airport. Screw having a car wait for her. I want to be there when she gets off the plane," Stu said, his voice picking up momentum.

"I like that. I like that idea," Jadon said, springing off the sofa.

"Let me call Erin, have her watch the dogs. We'll be cutting it close with the gig tonight, but who cares, man. We'll just stroll in and rock the fucking place then get the hell out of there. I'm freaked out. Jesus, I feel like at any minute there will be gunfire again," Chick said, calling Erin.

Chapter 13

"Hand me the next bag," Chick said, reaching down toward Bob. "It'll all fit. No worries. These things are made to carry a ton."

Pushing down forcefully on the over-filled cargo box sitting atop the black GMC Yukon XL Denali, that he had delivered to his house that morning from the rental agency, Chick realized it wasn't going to close without a fight. Putting his cigarette in the corner of his mouth, he pushed hard with both hands until hearing a loud snap.

"Got it." Chick looked down at the faithful flock gathered early in his driveway. "Let's get the fuck out of Dodge," he said, jumping off the running board and landing with a thud next to Erin.

Meg repositioned her arm inside her sling before giving an appreciative smile to Chick. Looking at the disheveled faces of the band, she felt guilty, knowing it was because of her that they were all suddenly taking this journey up through the mountains. After the band picked her up at the airport night before last, Jadon wasted no time filling her in on how they felt about Devon's sudden appearance. More startling was learning that John had flown to New York to watch over her.

"You all right?" Jadon asked, leaning his head in close to Meg's.

"Oh, yeah. Just feeling goofy. For the love of Pete, here we go, all because of me," Meg said, stretching her tight neck.

"It's not because of you. I mean . . ." Jadon stopped to find the right words.

"Nah. Meggie, we're just all spooked and needing some time to unwind. Maybe while we're trapped in this behemoth . . . ," Stu said, shooting a thumb in the direction of the huge SUV weighted down with cargo.

"Hey, it's the only thing short of one of those fucking homelier than shit passenger vans that would fit everyone, including two damn dogs," Chick interrupted, hoisting Lil' Larry into the back alongside Big Larry, who had already jumped inside.

"Like I was saying, while we're under Chickie's control, maybe we can coax your arm out of hibernation. And maybe give John time to figure out what the hell is going on," Stu said, sliding onto the front passenger seat while glancing back at Bob. "What? I called shotgun."

"No bickering," Chick said, helping Erin up into the second row seat of the Denali.

Putting her arm around Meg, Erin gave her a tight squeeze. "I think this sounds like a blast. When *don't* we need a break like this? I know I could use one. Who cares why we're taking off? As long as we're taking off."

"Yeah, who cares the reason? It's just cool to be road trippin' again," Bob said, leaning forward from the third row of seats.

Slamming the door closed beside him, Chick adjusted the rearview mirror and grinned as he looked back at the truck filled to the brim with smiling faces.

"Can't see the Larrys," Chick said, throwing a piece of gum into his mouth.

Both Bob and Kofi peered behind them at the two motley dogs busy trying to find comfort within their small surroundings.

"They could use more room. Well, Big Larry could. Lil' Larry already laid down," Kofi said, still watching Big Larry shuffle and scoot his pillow around.

Rubbing his hand across Meg's back, Jadon whispered softly, "Hey, we're just wanting to get away for a bit. Get you away from those moronic interviewers . . . the pressure surrounding all that. I guess we just feel a bit edgy. But it's not because of you."

"In a large way it is," Meg answered. "You said me running into Devon has you unsettled. And I understand. I don't trust him. But I have to say, he helped. And I needed it," Meg admitted, frustrated with the truth.

Hearing her words, Jadon rested his head against hers, wishing this would be one of the times Meg's cynicism would take over, not her hopefulness.

"I just don't feel right about it, Meg. I don't believe in coincidences. Devon is a bit too high on the food chain to go to those things, so why was he there?" Jadon asked.

"I don't know. I honestly don't remember if he used to go to those events or not. But maybe knowing I was going to speak . . . curiosity got the best of him. He said he could help with the legal mess that Trish doesn't seem to be successful at helping me with. He said to ask you . . . he said he knows he hurt a lot of people and doesn't expect forgiveness."

"Stu you got that conference on your phone. Don't you?" Bob asked.

"Yeah. I got it," Stu said, bringing up the YouTube video on his cell phone. "We admit he sounded sincere, Meggie, but he's one cunning ass slime ball."

"I wouldn't be surprised if he had that little speech rehearsed," Chick said, programming the GPS for the second time. "Everything in me says he is evil. Why else would John feel he needed to go watch out for you? Something's up. Not that anyone's heard from good ol' John Hastings yet. Christ."

Pushing harder than necessary on the flat screen of the navigational system, Chick finally nodded his head, pleased he'd entered their destination correctly.

"Got the water for the Larrys?" Chick asked once again, as he rolled the large truck down their long, winding driveway.

"Yes. We've covered this a million times. Both big and little Larry have plenty of water." Erin smiled.

"Sorry. It's been a while since we went on a road trip, and when we did, we didn't have any dogs, or pregnant women, or delicate stroke survivors along for the ride. Not to mention tired, middle-aged rockers ready to snap like a pile of dry twigs." Chick laughed at himself and the frazzled condition everyone was in as he pulled onto the road. "We've done world tours that haven't worn us out as much as the last few months have."

"I don't want to see it again," Flora said, giving the phone back to Kofi and Bob.

"What do you think?" Meg asked, turning to look behind her at Flora.

"All I can say, sweetheart, is something about it doesn't feel right. It feels right only in that it fits with Devon's energy. Honestly, and I know you don't want to hear this, I think he's up to something. But my mind has been on other things. It's only been recently that I've turned my focus back onto Devon. I know you're not in danger, Meg. But . . . I think anyone who goes against Devon . . . is," Flora said, rubbing her hand on Kofi's knee next to her.

Turning back around, Meg didn't like what she heard. She knew that people didn't change, but then again Devon said he hadn't changed. To believe there could be good in him was like believing in a fairytale, but as a writer, there's always the innate desire to believe that anything is possible. Resting her head on Jadon's shoulder, she tried to ignore the reality, instead she chose to let the fairytale float in the back of her mind like wispy clouds that if left alone could form into a large, believable mass.

Sliding a Lucky from its pack, Stu lit it in one, perfected, habitual motion.

"No smoking, dude. There's a baby in the Goddamn car!" Chick shrieked, snatching the long white cigarette from Stu's relaxed lip.

"Oh, yeah," Stu smiled at Erin. "I forgot. My bad."

"Jesus, that's the heir to the throne, dude. Just chew gum, like me," Chick said, opening the storage compartment between them revealing a treasure chest of gum.

"This is gonna be a fuckin' long ride," Stu snorted, looking out the window at the cars lining the freeway. "We're not going to be on the freeway the whole time, are we? GPS lady said to get in the right lane."

"I heard the directions. No need to repeat 'em. That was her first warning. We've got plenty of time," Chick said, snapping his gum.

Looking past Jadon, Meg watched the world lurch by. It was a world that moved quickly at times, then halted abruptly, giving her the opportunity to take note of the houses that had the misfortune of having a freeway for a backyard. Closing her eyes, Meg felt her body lulled to sleep by the rhythmic movements of the Denali struggling to make headway in the early morning traffic that moved away from the ocean and toward the mountains.

❦

With softened steps, Devon walked through Meg's house. Running his fingers across her laptop, he lifted the small glass paperweight sitting on her desk and remembered when he gave it to her. He was pleased she still kept it after all he had done. *If she abhorred me, she wouldn't want to stare at this,* he said to himself with a smile, slowly putting the glass bird back onto her desk.

Not wanting to be seen, he resisted the temptation to stand on her balcony. Instead he chose to walk into the bedroom. Standing at the foot of her bed, he smirked while taking a long, dissatisfied sigh and turned abruptly. He didn't want to linger in her bedroom. He could still smell Meg. The only problem was he could also smell Jadon.

Stopping at the doorway, he turned back and headed to the bedside table and slid open the drawer. Sliding its contents around, he lifted the notes and cards still left inside and smiled. Meg hadn't removed him completely from her life. A few cards he had sent her over the past still remained. Looking at the other bedside table, he wondered if Jadon had completely moved in, or was just enjoying Meg's bed.

Cautiously sliding the other bedside table drawer open, he groaned lightly. Everything inside appeared to be Jadon's. Taking the stack of loose leaf papers, Devon surrendered briefly to his hatred of Jadon and flipped the papers over, placed them back inside and slid the drawer closed.

Walking through the living room, he picked up the black and white photo prominently displayed on the table next to the sofa. He ran his finger along the silver frame as he stared at the woman. Breaking his gaze, he looked out the french doors leading to the balcony then back down at the beautiful blonde woman whose light colored eyes looked as though they were painted with water colors instead of formed by the often unforgiving mechanics of a camera.

"Still no photos of your mum, Meg," Devon said, putting the photo back in its place.

Walking to the kitchen, Devon stopped suddenly when his foot caused a large shrill squeal to fill the air. Looking down he noticed the angry stuffed cat he had inadvertently stepped on.

"Oh, that's right, we've moved on from Bob," he said unhappily.

Devon looked out the kitchen window and carefully eyed the beach house that sat too close to Meg's home.

"So that's *his* house," Devon whispered. "Well my dear Meg, at this stage of the game, the only thing I don't know about you, is when you'll be home."

With that Devon went back to Meg's desk and made himself comfortable. Thumbing through her calendar, Devon grinned, happy to see that Meg still preferred her paper calendar to the digital ones. Taking out his cell, he methodically added all of Meg's notes and appointments to his calendar.

Opening her eyes, Meg noticed the houses were still in their place. She lifted her head from Jadon's shoulder and gave him a tired smile.

"Hey, sleepy girl. Erin's out too," Jadon whispered, turning his eyes in Erin's direction. "You've been asleep for a while, but we've hardly moved."

"We had some serious gridlock for a while. Felt like we were stuck on fly paper back there," Chick said with a moan. "We wiggled and broke free though."

Looking at Jadon, Meg said softly, "I have to wonder if I should have published that last book under the name Kathleen Kelly. Life might have been easier. There would have been no appearances. Nothing. Maybe I made a mistake."

"No, you didn't" Flora said softly from behind her.

"No. I agree, you didn't make a mistake," Bob said affectionately. "This mess will get sorted out. You're just in new territory. With new challenges. You're not going to know what's behind the door until you open it . . . "

"Unless it's glass," Stu said, allowing his voice to express what his mind was envisioning. "Unless it's a glass door. Then you could see right through it."

"Well, life hasn't given me too many glass doors that I can remember," Bob shot back.

"Don't get touchy. I was just sayin' . . . that'd be a way of knowing what's ahead, what's behind the proverbial *door* . . . Just a fuckin' observation," Stu said, elevating his voice.

"Doesn't matter what the hell the door is made out of. In this case, it was oak. Solid oak," Bob said, raising his voice enough to wake Erin.

"I don't think it matters what the door is made of . . . ," Kofi said, trying to calm their bickering.

"Why the hell did the GPS lady say she's recalculating. Fuck. We missed our exit. Goddamn it. You two stop it!" Chick yelled, pushing the Denali through the traffic and into the right lane.

"I didn't hear her say anything," Stu grumbled.

Meg relaxed into Jadon's arms while he wrapped them around her like a blanket. Resting her head on his shoulder, she watched as they exited the freeway and moved onto a surface street. While they waited at a red light she stared at the homeless man sleeping next to his shopping cart. As the Denali powered forward, she looked at the large homes lining the boulevard and tried to make sense of the blend of affluence and poverty that was the backdrop of L.A.

"Go to sleep. There's nothing to see," Jadon said, rubbing his beard across the top of Meg's head.

"I was just thinking about my mom. She always thought it would be nice to spend time on the West Coast. But she never had the chance," Meg said.

"Speaking of moms, did you call your mom back?" Erin asked Chick.

"Nope," he answered.

"Whoa, Lavinia called?" Bob questioned. "Yikes."

"She never calls. I think he should call her back. But he won't," Erin said with a sigh.

"You never talk about your parents. Why?" Meg asked.

"Nothing to talk about," Chick said, turning onto the road leading into the San Bernardino Mountains.

"Lavinia wasn't what you would call a supportive parent," Stu snorted.

"This is my home," Chick said, twirling his finger in the air to show he meant the people sitting in the Denali with him. "Sometimes home isn't with your blood family. It's with the family life gives you once you break free."

The words struck Meg's heart hard; she never realized Chick had such a painful past. Looking at Erin for confirmation of her thoughts, Erin gave Meg a sad look.

"Jesus, do we all have messed up parents or childhoods?" Meg said with a chuckle to lighten the air.

"Pretty much," Stu said, sliding his pack of cigarettes back in his pocket. "Christ, I've slid these little monsters out of my pocket twenty times. When we stopping?"

"Kofi and Erin are the only ones who have parents that had their shit together," Chick said, answering Meg before Stu. "Once we're on this road for a while, we'll find a store or something. The Larrys might have to take a leak."

"Do I get to hear about them?" Meg asked, looking at Erin, then back at Kofi.

"There's not much to say," Erin said, sliding her back against the door and feet across Meg's lap. "My parents were just good people who gave me a good life. I guess it gives us hope that not everyone is messed up."

"Why are your ankles soft?" Meg said, massaging Erin's feet. "You're a long way from hatching the Holchick egg."

"Hmm . . . you shouldn't have pudgy ankles yet, Erin," Flora said, peering over Meg's shoulder. "How was your checkup?"

"All of her gauges read that she's running along great, except for her blood pressure. It was through the roof. Another reason why we're taking this little break. Mama bear's been getting upset too easy and too much. The doctor said she might blow a gasket if she doesn't take it easy," Chick said, the subject making him chew nervously on his gum.

Erin felt everyone turn and look at her with concern. "Obviously, that's not exactly what the doctor said. But, that is pretty much the gist of it. I just have to take it easy, that's all. And if it continues, then I might be confined to my bed. Not fun."

"How far along are you?" Meg asked.

"I'm just finishing week twelve," Erin beamed.

"Oh, yeah. We got arms, legs . . . we've got roughly three inches of baby growing back there so far," Chick said, his face showing every ounce of joy he felt about becoming a father.

"Someone's excited," Erin said proudly.

"Fuck, yeah. I'm ready. This kid's going to get everything I didn't. I'm going to believe in this little dude."

"Or dudette," Stu interrupted.

"Yeah, either way. I'm going to be their biggest cheerleader," Chick said, his eyes watering at the thought.

"You're going to make a wonderful father, Chick. I can see it," Flora said confidently.

Nodding his head, Chick liked what Flora said. There was no way he was going to shred the soul of his kid the way his mom shredded his. Some parents are physically abusive; Chick's mom was abusive in a completely different way. Instead of using a fist, she used her words. Regardless of how successful he was, he never forgot that to his mother he was a failure. That was one of the many reasons he had no plans of returning her call.

"Are you going to be surprised or find out beforehand if you've got a dude or dudette?" Kofi asked.

Chick looked in the rearview mirror at Erin. She answered with a shrug and a content smile.

Meg watched the excitement flow from their faces and listened as it washed over their words. Looking at Jadon, she tried to hold back the tears wanting to emerge from her sad eyes. She was tired of crying, and more than anything she didn't want to dampen Erin's joy. Although she was excited for Erin and Chick, the reality was that she would never have the opportunity to share that type of excitement with Jadon. Feeling her sadness, Jadon kissed her forehead. Keeping his mouth rested on her head, he slowly moved his mouth back and forth to soothe Meg's pain.

"Finally!" Stu said, once Chick finally turned off the winding mountain road and into the parking lot of a small store resembling something of an old mining town depot. "I need a smoke."

⁓

Looking through Meg's medical papers, Devon learned more than Arianna had been able to discover. As he relaxed in the large, white, overstuffed chair in the living room, he casually crossed his legs and rubbed his finger across his bottom lip while reading the doctor's notes from her last visit.

"*No progress with mobility.* That's not very promising," he said quietly, sliding out another piece of paper. "What is this . . . ?"

Engrossed in the prognosis notes listed on Meg's discharge papers, Devon jumped slightly when the telephone rang. Smiling at himself for being so on edge, he resumed reading the notes while the answering machine picked up.

"Jadon. It's your dad. Your message broke up at the end. I won't be back for a couple days. I'm following a lead. Take care of Larry. And Jay . . . I think Devon is close by. Watch Meg."

Devon's head rose slowly upon hearing the last two sentences.

"And who . . . pray tell . . . are you?" He whispered.

Placing the stack of papers on his crossed legs, Devon sat silently thinking. The realization that someone was on to him instantly overwhelmed him. It was a feeling completely foreign to Devon, as normally he eased through all situations without any hindrances or obstacles, only because he arranged things to fall into place that way.

Devon raked his long fingers through his dark hair. It was apparent that he had an adversary. And from the sound of the voice on the answering machine, one who presented a very real threat to his plans. Jadon had never caused the hair on Devon's neck to stand on end, but the voice on the answering machine did.

Flustered, Devon placed Meg's discharge papers and notes from her last check-up back on her desk. Staring at the phone he impulsively dialed *69, causing the phone to dial the last call received. Pushing the speakerphone button, he listened to the repetitive ring. He waited patiently, but no one picked up on the other end.

⁓

Looking at his cell phone, John noticed Meg's home telephone number scrolling across the screen. Considering that less than a few minutes ago he'd heard enough of Jadon's message to know that at the present moment they weren't home, he wondered who was calling from their house. John answered, but once he did, the call disconnected.

Tossing his cell phone on the writing desk in his motel room, John reprocessed his thoughts, making certain he heard Jadon correctly. He would have saved the message had it not been so garbled. But he heard enough to know they were gone for a few days, and they had the dogs.

After placing a quick call, he threw a handful of ice into a glass and poured out the last of his whiskey. His friend at the station would pass along the message, and soon an unmarked car would patrol Meg's house. If anything didn't look right, they would investigate and he'd receive a call. Until then, John would resume his search for the litigious Mr. Strum, the unknown author who claimed Meg stole his manuscript and used it for her latest book. Something in John's gut told him that there was more to this lawsuit than a bottom feeder trying to extort money. Like an oil painting found at a garage sale, John knew the image displayed on top was just a cover; if his instincts were right, buried beneath where the brush strokes that formed a masterpiece of deception.

Chapter 14

Sliding across the long, wooden bench seat at the Gold Nugget Grill, Meg made room for Jadon, Erin and Chick; all of which sat across from Stu, Flora, Kofi and Bob on the other side of the table. At the sound of the waitress's voice, all eight looked up in unison and listened to the specials the small country diner offered that evening.

Once the waitress left, Stu looked across the table at Meg. "This is a one fork establishment, simple food. Whatever you do, remember the rules of being on the road."

Meg looked at everyone, then back at Stu.

"Believe me, never order buffalo wing chicken salad while on the road. It's one of those things ya learn the hard way. Like breaking wind while standing in the shower, once you do it, you try to never do it again," Stu said flatly.

"Do you really have to talk that way before we order?" Bob said in disgust. "How the hell are we suppose to pick out anything thinking about that horrible episode you had years ago?"

"Oh . . . it was bad," Stu groaned in a low whisper while sinking behind his large, plastic menu.

"I think it had more to do with the mayonnaise than anything else," Erin said, scrunching her nose. "We all still have nightmares from the horrible hours that followed after he ate that."

"We barely made it to the gig. We were stopping at every Goddamn tree and gas station from here to Barstow," Chick said, not lifting his head from behind his menu.

Stu looked at Meg with a contorted face. "It was bad," he whispered.

"Enough," Bob ordered.

"Boys," Flora said.

"Moving on . . . ," Chick said, trying to turn the conversation. "Who's beeping?"

Everyone looked at their phones, but only Meg and Jadon had messages.

"My dad called back. I don't have a signal," Jadon said, wondering if his dad had any news or was being his normal elusive self.

"Devon sent me a text," Meg said, opening the message.

MEG, I HOPE YOU MADE IT BACK SAFELY. I HAVE, AS PROMISED, SUSPENDED THE PRESS PASSES OF THE REPORTERS WHO ACTED INAPPROPRIATELY. ALSO, I HAVE CONFIRMED WITH TRISH TO POSTPONE FURTHER PUBLICITY ENGAGEMENTS UNTIL YOU FEEL READY AND ABLE. IF I CAN BE OF ANY FURTHER HELP OR ASSISTANCE, PLEASE KNOW, I WILL. YOU NEED ONLY TO ASK. PLEASE BE SO KIND AS TO TELL ME YOU ARE DOING WELL. I LOOK FORWARD TO YOUR RESPONSE.

Looking up, Meg saw seven faces waiting. Reading the message to everyone, she awaited their response.

"I don't know what the hell to think anymore. I think he's trying . . . ," Meg paused.

"Trying to what?" Bob asked. "God, I just wish we knew more about the publishing world. Then we could better help you. You don't need him, Meg, you really don't."

"I know. I know. Trish had been getting real pushy, but . . . this must be why she recently backed off and said to *get better*. I was kind of hoping she softened up all on her own. I guess not."

"Don't tell him where you are," Flora said.

Because the words came from Flora, Meg felt her stomach flip. "Why? I mean, what difference does it make?"

"I don't know," Flora answered. "I guess it doesn't. The words just flew out of my mouth."

Looking at his cell, Stu mumbled. "Hey, Jay, I got a few bars. Want to use my phone to call John back?"

Jadon plucked the cell phone from Stu's hand before he finished his last word, and Erin and Chick were already sliding out of the booth so Jadon could go outside. Whether they came from Flora or John, everyone was eager for answers.

Pacing outside the small diner, Jadon waited for his dad to pick up on the other end.

"Dad, it's Jay."

Listening to his father, Jadon tried to position the cell phone so he didn't miss any words. Once he heard his father's voice loud and clear, he cemented his feet in one place.

"No, we aren't home. The band, Erin, Flora . . . we all took off. We fuckin' freaked out because we didn't know what the hell was going on. We have the dogs, too. Meg said she didn't see you in New York. Did you do that on purpose or did you miss her? What?" Jadon waited, listening to John. "No, we left early this morning, before 8:00 a.m. We're heading up Mill Road. No, we don't have anyone at the house. Why?" he asked, then waited. "You what? Fuck. That's not good."

Pacing in circles, Jadon began to lose reception again, but his nerves required movement.

"Okay, call me and let me know if they see anything."

Ending the call, Jadon shot back in the diner and slid next to Meg.

"What the fuck's going on, Jay? Christ, you don't look good," Stu asked, not taking his eyes off Jadon's ashen face.

Taking a deep sigh, Jadon didn't want to worry Meg or upset Erin. Because there were no answers yet, he would only be adding to the heightened anxiety everyone already felt.

"Uh, he just said he won't be back for a while, and asked if I could keep Larry. You know my dad. He always seems so elusive. He just gets to me," Jadon said, taking a long drink of water.

Noticing Chick's eyes weren't turning away from his face, Jadon slowly looked back at him. Eye to eye with Jadon, Chick could tell something had taken a sinister turn. Grabbing his cell phone, Chick pounded out his question.

Hearing his phone beep from a message received, Jadon took his cell phone from his pocket, and read Chick's message. He looked out the window, then back at his phone, before typing a quick answer that he sent to everyone except the two he worried most about, Meg and Erin.

> JOHN RECEIVED A CALL FROM MEG'S HOUSE
> JUST MINUTES AGO. AND, AN HOUR AFTER
> MEG FLEW BACK TO LA , SO DID DEVON.

Sliding his phone back in his pocket, Chick didn't say a word; neither did Stu, Bob, Kofi or Flora.

"I don't want to go back," Jadon said, kissing Meg on the cheek.

"Is John okay? You look like you've seen a ghost," Meg asked.

"I'm good. Did you get any other messages?" Jadon said, looking at Meg's phone resting on the table.

"Ugh, yeah. An e-mail from Trish. She said this weirdo George Strum is getting aggressive with his legal bullshit. I need to find a different attorney. The one Trish recommended is a money pit. And the one the band uses is busy. Now what?" Meg said, looking around the table. "I just want this guy to go away."

❧

In their rustic motel room, darkened by the late hour and its remote location buried in the mountains, Jadon curled behind Meg on their bed and held her tight.

"I'm glad Chick called it a night. I'm tired. And I wanted to be alone with you," Jadon said, letting his words fall softly into Meg's ear.

Turning onto her back, she looked at his beautiful face, in doing so she smiled knowing she would never tire of looking at him, nor would there be a time when her heart didn't skip a beat when her eyes met his. All of her life, through every novel she wrote, she hoped to experience the love she felt for Jadon. But never once during all of her dreaming did she expect the talons of struggle that constantly wrapped around their love.

"I didn't want to devour you in front of everyone," he whispered.

Meg smiled. "I needed to be alone with you, too. I feel like I've waited a lifetime to be with you. Even though there is this flurry of activity bustling around us, the core of me is grounded in this unshakable love . . . and desire. It's pretty weighty stuff," she said, laughing at herself and how emotional her words were.

Sliding on top of Meg, Jadon kissed her lips, then her eyelids, pulling his head back he smiled, but not from happiness alone. Instead it was a smile of safety. For the first time in his life, he felt there was a safety net below him, waiting for him in case he fell. Even though it was Meg who seemed to be teetering on the tightrope, he couldn't shake the feeling that soon he would be standing toe to toe with Devon.

"Meg, during that press conference they mentioned my drug problems. Yet you haven't asked me about it," Jadon said softly.

"No, I haven't. I don't care. I only want to hear what you want to tell me. Nothing . . . will change how I feel about you. My love isn't like the waves. It doesn't roll in and out at varying levels. My love for you . . . is like the deep waters far out in the ocean. It's unchanging."

Resting his forehead gently on her nose, he sighed hearing the beautiful words and the truth he knew shaped them.

"I used them to escape the things I couldn't change. The past," he said, looking up at Meg. "It didn't work.

It didn't change anything, except the more I tried, the worse my mind became and the more intense my body protested stopping. Like dominoes, once the first one fell, the rest fell fast, and hard."

"What happened to make you stop?"

"Almost dying. Sort of had a profound effect on me," he stopped and tilted his head to one side, releasing a chuckle to hide the close call he had. "Although I'm not sure why it scared me straight. I mean, I was considering dying as a possible way out. But something told me it wasn't my time to die. So I held on," Jadon said, running his hand through his hair before looking down at Meg, causing his long blonde strands to dust across her face.

"God, I'm glad you listened and held on," Meg said, reaching up and softly pulling with her teeth on Jadon's lower lip, coaxing his mouth to open and his body to respond to hers.

Opening his eyes, Jadon took advantage of the image resting before him. As if painted on a moving canvas, he watched Meg turn down the volume in her mind. He watched as she listened instead to her soul as it connected physically with his. Kissing her deeply, he closed his eyes briefly as he always did. Within her kisses, the constant reminders of the world around him diminished. Much like the doorway created from drugs that allowed him to step out of his body, within Meg he felt the same intoxication and release from the world.

Holding Meg tight, he turned onto his back and pulled her body on top of his. He paused, then ran his hands along her thighs and onto her hips, while staring into her eyes, mesmerized by the spectrum of gold and green that lit them like precious stones polished to brilliance.

"You hold on, through whatever happens," Jadon said, running his hand up the small of Meg's back. "I can't lose you."

Lowering her chest onto his, Meg's red hair created a canopy surrounding his face. "I'm not going anywhere," she whispered into his open mouth.

⤛

Looking down at the small pile of cigarette butts scattered next to his feet, Chick turned and mindlessly read the neon sign sitting prominently on the roof of the Mountain Motel. He cast a quick glance behind him and noticed how the sign projected a green hue onto the parking lot and the surrounding pine trees. Twisting his foot on top of another cigarette butt, within a half hour's time he tried to make up for a day of not smoking. When he heard the small crunch of footsteps on gravel behind him, he turned quickly.

"Hey," Jadon said.

Jadon lit a Lucky and took a deep inhale as he leaned his body against the Denali. Looking up at the stars he exhaled slowly.

"That text was fucked. What the hell is going on? Am I paranoid? Tell me I'm paranoid," Chick said, leaning next to Jadon.

"I don't know what to think. I'm wondering if it was Devon who called from the house. How's that for paranoid?" Jadon said, giving a nod to Bob, as soon as he saw him step outside the motel with the dogs.

"The dudes were whining," Bob said, releasing a yawn. "Give me one. I left my pack inside."

"Where's Stu?" Chick asked.

"He's out cold. He was babbling constantly about your text, took a few hits then crashed. It's probably for the best. I'm getting worried about him. He's smoking countless packs a day. He was about to explode on the ride up here," Bob said, holding his cigarette in the corner of his mouth as he led the dogs to the trees bordering the parking lot.

"He's worried," Jadon said, flicking the ashes from his cigarette. "We're all worried. I didn't want to say anything. It would upset Meg even more. I don't know anything about blood pressure, but I can't imagine stress helps, so I didn't want Erin to know. Fuck. We don't *know* anything really."

"What are the chances that all of this means nothing?" Bob asked. "Nothing at all? And we're all just freaked from the stunts Devon pulled in Europe? I mean, I know that's what Meg wants to believe."

"My gut is telling me that Devon has to do with everything," Chick said flatly.

Bob questioned, "Yeah but, all those reporters, the questions they were asking. I mean, I don't like the guy.

I hope to God we never see him again, but how could that be connected with him?"

Jadon tossed his cigarette on the ground and covered it slowly and methodically with his foot. "He was just lying in wait. That's what he did. Like a fuckin' spider, he is waiting. I can tell he is waiting. I don't know how much of this has to do with him. But you will not convince me that he's not waiting and watching."

"Yeah, that we know, he's waiting. Like in a game of chess," Chick said.

"Yeah, and I'm the one he's waiting on more than Meg," Jadon said. "He's waiting for me to make a wrong move. And I don't even know how to move. I don't even know how to fucking play chess. And he's a champion at it. Our lawyer is busy, so he can't help with this idiot Strum. And the guy Trish does hire is an asshole. It's like he tries to hide his fucking incompetence by being such a blow-hard ass bag that you can't hardly think straight. Meg can't stand him. Then suddenly Devon steps in and instantly Meg's publishing company *allows* her time to collect herself. That's not a coincidence. That's Devon."

Jadon slid another cigarette from its pack, lit it, and let out an overwhelmed breath. "Yeah, we can fill a stadium. People scream and think we're fucking great. But none of that does one thing to help Meg with this. You saw that video from the book fair. He walked up there . . . and you could tell he owned that place. He was like Moses. He stretched out his arms to quiet everyone, and the fucking Red Sea parted."

"Yeah, and what's that about his company having ties to the music industry? Those were the words that made my gut tighten," Bob said, untangling the two dogs.

Shaking his head, Chick looked hard at the stars dotting the sky above them. "We just have to watch everything. I may sound like a nervous ninny, but I think he would take us all out in a heartbeat. But I have a feeling Meg is so overwhelmed that..."

"What?" Jadon asked.

Looking at him, Chick winced before continuing. "I just think she wants it all to go away, all the problems.

Mainly so she can be with you, once and for all. I just think she'd shake hands with Satan to be with you. And I'm just feeling real nervous inside that she might. She is tough, she'd go nose to nose with a dragon. I don't think she'd hide from him. I'm just saying she's been fucked with too much. If she felt it meant your life would be easier, I think she'd allow Devon in. I don't know, don't listen to me. Maybe I'm just tired. And I know she is too. We all are."

⟨⟩

Leaning his elbow out the open window of his truck, John squinted into the Southern California sun while pushing his cell phone hard against his ear. He didn't want to miss a word; on the other end, was an old friend at the police department.

"All I can say is, the guy didn't have much steam. Then suddenly he has a lawyer who either doesn't care if he gets paid or . . . Strum instantly won the lottery and can pay this guy. You know how lawyers are, John. They aren't exactly the most generous group. I can't get into Strum's bank records, not legally, you know that, but . . . lawyers sure as hell aren't known for their benevolence," the voice on the end of the line said with a chuckle.

"What do you know about this lawyer?" John asked, leaning back into the seat of his truck.

"Well, what do you wanna know? I mean . . . he wears a suit, shows up, and seems to push enough papers through the courts to keep this thing expensive. Not sure if any of it is productive. A lot seems to get canceled before it gets before the judge. Looks like a circus show, if you ask me."

"Anything else?" John asked.

"Nah, nothing of any importance. You have the info on where this guy lives. Which is another reason why I'm wondering how he could pay this lawyer. Let me put it this way, John: this lawyer, the one he suddenly switched to . . . he ain't wearing suits from JC Penney, if you know what I mean. Yet Strum lives in a shack in the woods of Northern California. Something about that seems screwy. Hey, I gotta run. You need anything. Just call. Take care, John. Good to know you're still around."

Flipping his phone closed, John rolled out of LAX and into the tight line of traffic bordering the airport, then quickly moved onto the freeway heading to Bay City. As he always did, John replayed the words he just heard, making sure they were cemented in place before adding his own.

Despite the warm air, and the turbulence it created, John kept his window down. With his arm resting on the sill and his hand tapping on his outside mirror, he tried to reason with his gut. True, enough information had been downloaded into his mind to prove something wasn't right. But he couldn't connect what his mind knew with what his instincts kept telling him. Right now, Meg was the only thing connecting the dots. Strum could have borrowed the lawyer's fee from family or friends, promising a big payback once he won his legal fight. But Strum didn't have any family. And as for friends, short of following him, there was no way of knowing.

Meditating to the methodical rhythm of tires rolling across pavement, John began to put in order that which he knew, from that which he didn't; in doing so, hoping to discover that he'd overlooked the obvious. As the minutes gathered into a small cluster creating an hour of time, John felt certain he hadn't missed anything. Nothing had been overlooked, yet there were large gaps separating everything that felt terribly wrong with the situation.

Give it time, give it time, he said to himself. John wasn't a gifted musician like his son, but he had a gift for seeing a problem before the problem was ready to reveal itself to everyone else. Grabbing his phone, he sighed and dialed Jadon.

≈

Dipping his paddle down hard into the river, Stu shared his thoughts. "See, now let's say you had been tempted to order something mysterious last night at the diner . . . like a buffalo wing chicken salad sandwich, for example. Or, let's say for the sake of the discussion...one of their many 'specials.' Cuz' ya gotta watch our for those specials, that's usually how a place tries to unload old food. Anyway, you would be locked up in your hotel room right now, and would have had to miss this *wonderful* opportunity to gaze at nature," he said, with a grumbling chuckle, and hand extended toward the treetops.

"Hey, watch it. Don't diss Mother Nature. You do, and we'll get caught in a downpour," Chick said, whipping his head behind him at the canoe holding Bob and Stu.

"Just messin' with ya, Chickie. You gotta lighten' up. All that stress is bad for your heart," Stu moaned, causing Bob to turn and threaten him with his canoe paddle. "Am I wrong?"

Jadon smiled at the familiar yet comforting dialogue being exchanged as they moved steadily down the river and glided past Bob and Stu. Turning around, Meg watched as the canoe holding the two slightly disheveled men and the two white dogs was left in last place.

"It's the damned dogs. They weigh us down!" Bob yelled.

"Ha! Unlikely my friend," Chick howled, throwing out one of many smiles he had finally felt comfortable giving that day. "The cooler in Flora and Kofi's canoe weighs a ton and they're long gone. I can't even see them anymore."

"Ah, it's cuz they're nature people," Stu grumbled, wiping the small beads of sweat from his forehead. "Phew, it's kinda hot out here."

"When did Kofi learn how to maneuver a canoe like that . . . ?" Bob wondered out loud.

"He figured it out over the last decade while you and I were out getting tattooed and drunk," Stu said, running his fingers though his short, golden hair. "Chick! We there yet?"

"We don't need any kids, we already have them. They're following us," Chick whispered to Erin, flicking a few droplets of water onto her.

"Oh, no, those aren't our kids. Ha! No way," Erin smiled.

The trees bordering the river allowed for only broken streams of light to shoot randomly across the river as the four canoes peacefully made their way down its winding path. Once the paddlers realized their destination was farther than expected, their voices grew silent, as if their bodies knew to squander what was left of their energy

Like a song, the paddles dipped repeatedly into the water until the sound of Kofi's canoe scraping across the stones and dirt could be heard.

"FUCK, YEAH!" Stu shouted, relieved they made it to their first stop.

Turning to look at Jadon, Meg pointed at his pocket. "You're buzzing."

Staring at her, Jadon tried to understand what she was talking about, "Oh, God, my phone. *Now* we have reception," he laughed.

⤙

Sliding his phone into his pocket, John realized he hadn't said much, but he felt good having shared what he did know with Jadon. And by the sound of it, everyone was safe and sound up in the mountains. He couldn't help but smile, thinking how Chick often used the mountains as a place to escape with the band. To John, the mountains were like a parent, waiting to nurture him and provide him with comfort when he returned home. The mountains breathed, just as he breathed. He never needed people while he was in the mountains, which most likely was why he went there after Emily's death. Every morning he enjoyed drinking coffee while sitting on his front porch and listening to the trees. Just like hearing the stories told by visiting friends, the trees with their rustling branches spoke of all they had seen during the night. In the evening he would listen to the owls, and during the day he would listen to the hawks. Either way, he always had company. And that company tried to remind him he wasn't alone. But without Emily, he knew he always was.

Turning onto Mandalay Bay Drive, John watched as a black BMW with dark windows pulled away from the curb outside Meg's house. Keeping his distance, he followed as the car casually made its way downtown and into the circle drive in front of the Hathaway Grand Hotel. John rolled his truck to a stop on the side of the street and watched as Devon stepped out.

Chasing Nirvana

Chapter 15

Dropping her small duffel bag on the floor, Meg felt a glimmer of rejuvenation, just as Chick said she would before whisking them off into the mountains three days ago. She was tired, but a good tired — the kind of tired that reminds the brain that it did something fun for a change. Meg kicked the bag to the side, making way for Jadon, who had a large duffel bag in his arms and Lil' Larry on a leash. Meg turned to see where Big Larry was.

"He's still in the car. He didn't want to come out," Jadon said, giving Meg a kiss on the cheek. "I left the door open. He knows where to go."

Meg laughed at the battle of wills taking place. Walking into the living room, she opened the French doors, allowing the ocean to become part of her home. She glanced across the kitchen and back at the living room. Looking long and hard at her writing desk, her smile disappeared. Staring at it, she tried to remember how she had left things.

"What's wrong?" Jadon asked, hugging Meg from behind.

"Nothing, I guess," she said.

"What? Something seem wrong?" Jadon asked, his heart taking a quick jump.

More than anything Jadon wanted to believe there was a technical problem that led his dad to believe someone made a call from their house while they were gone. But looking at Meg while she stared at her desk then around the room, Jadon felt his stomach tighten.

"It's probably nothing," Meg laughed at herself. "You know, ever since my house on Martha's Vineyard was broken into . . . now, if anything ever seems out of place, my mind goes there first. To the break-in. Then I have to think, and think, and think, trying to remember how I left things. And eventually I'll remember that I was the one that turned something off or on, or moved something. It's maddening. But, it's a part of me now. Full-on paranoia is ingrained in every cell of my body. But, for some reason, I could have sworn I left things differently on my desk. I honestly hadn't wanted to look at the doctor's prognosis and litany of warnings . . . so I've been purposely turning these papers face down. They're face up. Did you do that?" she said, turning to look at Jadon.

"No. No, I didn't," Jadon said, stepping back to look around the house.

Trying to remain calm, Jadon looked over everything, room to room. It was obvious there wasn't anything that stood out of place, nothing there now that wasn't there before. *Oh my God, what if he planted a bug? I don't even know what one looks like,* Jadon said to himself.

Meg walked slowly throughout the house, her body moving forward as if in a fog as she tried to shake off her uneasiness. From what she could remember everything was exactly as it should be; nothing had been changed, nothing had been taken. Sitting on her bed, she sighed deeply and glanced at her side table.

Pulling the drawer open she eyed its contents with suspicion. *Everything's normal. Get hold of yourself, Meg,* she said slowly within her mind as she walked back into the living room.

"Why are you looking behind the sofa pillows?" Meg asked.

"No reason," Jadon said, looking up abruptly.

Looking at the photo of Jadon's mother, Meg noticed that she needed to dust more often. The noticeable outline of where the frame normally stood on the end table screamed of her lazy housekeeping habits.

"Meg?" Jadon called from the bedroom.

"Hmm?" She said, standing in the doorway, repositioning her arm inside the sling.

"Did you do this?" Jadon said, looking down at the papers turned over inside the drawer.

❧

Looking first at the late hour displayed on her kitchen clock, then at the duffel bags from their trip still sitting by the door, Meg turned her blank eyes onto Flora and smiled unhappily. "*Fine* can mean many things. Oh . . . you look *fine*. It never means you look good or great. It means you're just shy of looking unacceptable. Fine can mean anything, from barely acceptable to not so bad. It's vague. And right now I don't feel fine, not even the barely acceptable kind."

"Well, it's what I know. You'll be fine. Maybe my definition of fine is different than yours," Flora sighed. "If I could get a clearer picture beyond that, I'd tell you."

"That's all right. I hardly know what to do with the things you *are* able to tell me," Meg said, pulling her right arm tight across her chest.

"John didn't find anything?" Erin asked, even though she had already asked the question shortly after walking in the door.

"He wasn't home. I don't know why Jadon called all you guys over. I think he's feeling edgy. He's convinced someone was in the house. Devon. He's convinced Devon was in the house," Meg said, letting her words trail off.

Walking back into the house, Jadon let his steps lead him directly to Flora. "Do you feel anything with this? Am I crazy?" He asked, tilting his head slightly with question.

"No, you're not crazy. I feel him here. I do. But I so dislike him, I'm worried that I'm letting it interfere with things. But I feel him. I feel him all around here. And it isn't a good feeling," Flora said, giving Jadon a soft look of sadness.

Flora knew her words were a mix of what Jadon wanted to hear and didn't want to hear. As she looked at Meg, Flora felt her stomach swirl with unhappiness. Rubbing her hand across Erin's back, she needed to feel something better. If she were going to be of any help to anyone, she needed to detach from the pain and frustration she was feeling.

"Well, that is fucking unsettling. Christ," Chick said, wanting to deal with Flora's words as blatant facts, not psychic intuition.

"I still think all of this is a bit over the top," Meg said. "I just had a feeling some of my things were moved. And Jadon says his notes and papers were turned over. That doesn't seem to justify everyone getting so worked up. I've been dealing with that type of paranoia ever since my old house was broken into. Paranoia is my middle name. But, it's not because it's warranted." She threw herself down onto the sofa, overwhelmed and unsettled.

"Guys," Flora said, looking at Chick, Bob, Jadon and Raffi. "Fill in the blanks . . ."

"Damn it all to hell," Stu interrupted loudly, slamming the front door closed behind him with his foot, and unhooking Larry's leash from his collar. "Larry didn't pick up on anything. I don't think anyway, hard to tell. Then again, he isn't exactly the sniffing breed. He's not a bloodhound. Come to think of it; his snout is all smooshed, like he ran into a wall. That can't be good for sniffing." Stu looked up and instantly changed his thought pattern. "What? What's going on?"

Meg scanned everyone's face. "What? What is it I don't know?"

Jadon stared at Stu, then back at Meg. "My dad received a call from here while we were gone. While we were in the Denali heading up the mountains, our phone number came up on his caller ID."

"What? Why . . . ," Meg stammered

"We didn't want to upset you. We didn't want to upset Erin. And because we don't know for sure who made the call, we thought it was best to not . . . ," Bob tried to explain.

"You are delicate, babe," Chick said, looking at Erin. "I didn't want your blood pressure shooting through the roof."

"I'm not delicate," Erin said flatly.

"You are to me," Chick said.

"The whole thing has us all riled up," Bob added. "We didn't want to get you two upset."

"Can that kind of thing happen by mistake? Like a glitch in the phone line or something?" Meg asked.

"That's what we were hoping," Jadon said. "But did you know Devon is here? In town?" He pointed downward to emphasize his question.

Meg shook her head. "No. He never said anything about coming out here."

"Still, how would he get in?" Erin asked.

"Why would he come here?" Meg added.

"The why is easy," Chick said. "*You.*"

"But how . . . you locked everything, right?" Bob repeated Erin's question.

"Oh, God," Meg whispered. "He still has a key."

Chasing Nirvana

Chapter 16

With guarded movements, Devon cautiously pulled back the sheer curtain draped across the window of his hotel suite. Looking down at the busy city street, he scanned for any suspicious vehicles. Letting out a soft chuckle, he shook his head and turned back around. Ever since hearing the message on Meg's answering machine, he felt as though he were being shadowed, even though thus far he hadn't seen anyone. Nonetheless, someone out there knew his name and knew he was in Bay City. Regardless of seeing anyone or not, the thought shadowed him constantly.

Easing himself into the leather chair that allowed him to look out over the balcony, Devon considered how carefully he had covered his tracks. There was only one task he planned to carry out personally; other than that he made certain to never let the left hand know what the right hand was doing. He held his missions separate from one another, knowing full well if ever the two hands were to meet they could easily overpower him. Knowledge is power — all the more reason he never let anyone know what anyone else was doing.

Devon smiled and closed his cell phone, pleased with how the legal issues were playing out. Blake Wilson, Director of the board of directors at Langly Communication in Toronto, was the perfect man to carry out the tasks required.

Their relationship wasn't well known, as so few knew of their time spent together in prep school. However, over the course of many years Blake had called upon Devon for help, personal and professional; providing Devon with an open door when he needed someone to assist George Strum with his claim of copyright infringement.

Right on schedule Blake was about to apply more heat, per Devon's instructions. Thus far Meg hadn't felt pressured to request Devon's help on the issue, but once things were allowed to burn wildly, Devon's hope was that she would seek out any way available to contain the fire. And as longstanding friends do, Blake never felt it necessary to ask why the flame was necessary or for what end. It would be in poor taste to ask for details as both men knew Devon could easily do the same to Blake. And with Blake's propensity for very young women, questions were effortlessly kept silent.

With quiet contemplation he reviewed the mental script displayed in his mind. Confident his efforts would provide the outcome needed, Devon dialed Jadon's number.

⚰

"Hey!" Jadon shouted, motioning for the big, white boxer to stay out of the ocean. "Larry! Get over here."

Looking at Jadon as if to double check the seriousness of the warning, Larry backed away from the water and returned to Jadon's side.

With his mind distracted by rampant thoughts, Jadon responded slowly to his cell phone when it buzzed repeatedly. Sliding his phone from his pocket, he glanced at the unfamiliar number.

"Hello."

"Good morning, Jadon," Devon paused, purposely adding time for the unexpected mind-spinning effect he felt certain he was causing. "I hope my call hasn't alarmed you."

"And to what do I owe this pleasure?"

"I want to offer my assistance. As I'm sure you're aware Meg is embroiled in a certain amount of legal troubles. Troubles I feel are not helping her in her recovery."

"We're handling them just fine."

"From what I hear, they're not being handled at all, or at least not competently," Devon said, slightly disappointed that he wasn't being offered the slightest verbal challenge.

"We'll be just fine," Jadon said, biting back his outrage.

"As everyone is brutally aware, Jadon, hiring the wrong attorney is often worse than the legal trouble that warranted the attorney. Surely you realize the globe is riddled with incompetent attorneys. I would hate to see Meg suffer any further. And I would think that you, of all people, would want her troubles lessened as well."

"Everything about *you* is trouble."

"Hardly. However, all I can do is offer my help and appeal to you as someone, like yourself, who cares deeply for Meg. If you care as much as you say you do, it seems only sensible that you would put your own feelings aside. Nevertheless, you do as you choose. I had hoped, however, that if we came to a truce of sorts we could eliminate the roadblocks encumbering Meg's recovery. If you change your mind, you now have my number."

Jadon flipped shut his phone, ending the call. Discussing things with Devon had never been an option; asking for his help felt much like kissing the back of Satan's hand. Looking out across the ocean, he wondered if Fate would be so wicked as to ever require him to kneel in Devon's direction.

Jadon turned his gaze onto the sand and wondered if he were being selfish. It was obvious Meg was sinking deeper and deeper into a level of depression, and painfully, he knew her hand was slowly losing its grip onto his. Her reasons were obvious; yet he couldn't erase or even begin to right the wrongs. What's more, every time his eyes met hers, he saw a thick curtain slowly being drawn; it was fabric that draped her spirit, the very thing he loved most.

Leaning back onto the beach, Jadon closed his eyes and let the early morning breeze glide across his face. Filled with unsettled energy, he sat up and pulled his legs tight to his chest, dropping his head on his knees, he prayed. Not knowing to whom he was talking, or if anyone or anything was listening, he allowed the heartfelt requests to flow freely.

Dear God. I finally have her. But I'm losing her. You know I'm losing her. Bring her back. I've waited lifetimes . . . to be able to spend this one with her. Lifting his head, he let the wind pull his hair away from his face. *I'll give you anything. Just bring her back.*

⁓

Gliding her hand across the cool morning sheets that covered her bed, Meg smiled while staring at the wrinkled imprint left by Jadon; a reminder that, not so long ago, he'd been lying beside her. Touching the sheets, she could tell he hadn't been gone long. Meg rolled onto her back and looked at the ceiling. She tried to ignore the boulder of disappointment sitting inside her chest. Instead, she tried to think of only the things that brought a smile to her face: Jadon, her friends, the dogs. She was blessed. She knew she was blessed. Every time she let her mind notice all the things that weren't working, she felt like a pathetic child, one that chose to wallow in its own gloom.

But as hard as Meg tried, she couldn't ignore how twisted and ironic life seemed. With every move toward her dreams came a move toward more discomfort and pain. *How does anyone see past that?* Meg wondered as she sat up and gazed out the French doors of her bedroom.

"I have my life's love, but I no longer have two hands to hold him with. I found the courage to publish my work under my own name, and I can no longer write. I found the one man I want to have a family with, and I can't have children. I'm allowed into a group of talented musicians, and I can't play music anymore. And adding to that, every step I take toward dealing with people shows me that people are sick, lying sons of bitches. How the hell do I see past any of that?" Meg snorted quietly, pushing herself out of bed.

Leaning against the large glass doors that displayed the ocean like a picture frame that showcased its masterpiece, Meg tried to bite down the tears grappling to take over her face. She let her head fall softly onto the glass and tried to make sense of all the turns her life had taken, and why. Every time she let her mind fall onto figuring out the why, she felt her chest tighten and stomach sink.

"Pull it together, Meg," she said to herself.

But disappointment fit Meg like a well worn pair of jeans — comfortable and familiar only because they'd been worn so often. Nothing helped to make sense of, or ease the disappointment of, losing her parents so brutally and unexpectedly. Adding to that was the pain of watching her mother's suffering during the years leading to the violent car crash that finally set her mother free. Meg knew it wasn't how her mother would've wanted to be released from an unfilled life, but it was without question the way Fate had decided to end it.

The pain of losing her mother filled Meg with a consistent flow of loneliness. The only thing powerful enough to block the stream of loss was playing the violin, something she could no longer do. Standing alone in her room, she began to cry.

"No wonder so many people choose to check out early," Meg said bitterly. "God forbid anyone should be able to live their dream. Or maybe others do. Maybe. That sure doesn't seem to be my journey, though. God, what is going on?"

Running her hand through her hair, Meg spun around and began to pace. Her steps were put into motion by the forceful thrust of tears that repeatedly erupted from her chest.

"God, what is so wrong with wanting things to work out. Fuck. Fuck!" Meg screamed as she walked into the living room.

As her mindless steps moved her body in circles around the desk in her living room, Meg grew angrier. With every raspy sob, her footsteps moved steadily in the same circle as if on a mission. Every fiber in her body was enraged from the cruelty of not just her life but of the only life she had ever carefully watched play out — her mother's. Noticing that the beast that shadowed her mother also seemed to shadow her, Meg's sobs of pain turned to cries of anger.

Screaming into the air, Meg cursed the creature of powerlessness that sat inside her soul. Circling her desk, she cursed God. Her pace remaining steady, she cursed everything she thought life was suppose to be. She cursed the notion of hope. She cursed the sadistic theory of Fate. She cursed the images that played in her mind of her mother talking to her in that far off place, telling her that there was a reason for all things. She cursed her own mind for being so delusional for having bought into the idea that there was something larger at work in her life, something that was watching out for her and bringing it all together.

Letting out a mournful, violent cry, Meg cursed her dreams. Her final thought struck so deeply within her soul she felt her knees give way to the weight of her spirit having been cut down like a tree, forced to collapse hard onto the ground. Trying to keep herself from falling, she held onto her desk. Staring down at the papers stacked next to her laptop, her eyes read the doctor's orders, carefully detailing her inability to ever carry a child full term. With her head hung in defeat, she let her tears turn the hated words to a blur. In one abrupt motion Meg grabbed the glass paperweight sitting on her desk and sent it flying across the room. With her eyes closed, and her ears imprisoned by the sound of shattering glass, she fell to the floor.

"Meg?" Jadon said, standing in the doorway. "Meg!"

Collapsing his body behind hers, he pulled his arms around her small frame and tried to cover her body with his.

"Meg . . . ," he whispered into her ear. "You threw that with your right hand . . ."

⁂

Wiping his lips with the back of his hand, John put the small silver flask of whiskey back in the glove box. Allowing his back to sink into the seat of his truck, he sighed. Connecting the dots of a crime always took the longest. It was also the most maddening part of any investigation. John's gut solved most crimes within a few short days, sometimes quicker than that. It was getting the proof that took days, often longer, and unfortunately allowed many a guilty man to walk free.

Devon was guilty, that was clear. But of what exactly, John couldn't say. Yet he knew Devon was steadily carrying out a plan. And if John's gut proved correct, it was a plan that would destroy his son. John would easily allow himself to be destroyed before he would permit his son to be harmed. Like breathing, protecting Jadon required no thought.

Giving Larry a rub along the back that caused the stocky bulldog to let out a long moan, John looked back over the street address sitting in front of him. There were no obvious connections between George Strum and Devon Hathaway, yet everything inside of him told him there was a steady line of ink, even if unseen by the naked eye.

Chapter 17

"What's going on man?" Chick said, closing the door to the studio behind him with his foot. "I couldn't tell by your message if things had gotten better . . . or worse."

"Better, things are better," Jadon said, looking up from the sofa.

"There's my guy," Bob said, softly pushing his words through a smile while plopping down on the sofa and motioning for Larry to jump in his lap.

"We're all ears, dude. Spill it," Chick said, nervously lighting up a cigarette.

"Slide, Clyde," Stu said, motioning for Bob to make room for him on the sofa.

"Can't you sit over there?" Bob motioned with his head at the chair.

"No. I don't want to sit in the fuckin' hand chair. Just pick up Larry's butt and I'll slide under," Stu said, not taking no for an answer.

Staring at Bob and Stu, then back at Chick, Jadon began, "First, and the most important thing . . . Meg used her right hand."

"Yes!" Chick shouted, throwing his hands in the air.

"Oh, man, finally, Goddamn. That is good news," Bob said, letting his head fall back onto the sofa in relief.

"Meggie must be beside herself," Stu smiled, leaning over Larry's large white body to grab a cigarette from its pack.

"Well . . . she thinks I just saw what I wanted to see. But I know what I saw. She was having a breakdown. A pretty bad one. I walked in with Big Larry and I watched her pick up this glass paperweight from her desk and whip the fucking thing clear across the room. She shattered the picture on the wall," Jadon said.

"She doesn't remember doing it?" Chick asked.

"No. It was so fast. It was just instinct, I think. Which means her body is ready. She has a roadblock, but it isn't her body. It's her mind."

"This is still fucking great news man. This is awesome. This is fucking awesome," Chick said, jumping up with anxious energy. Spinning around, he looked at Jadon. "What's not so great then?"

"Devon called me," Jadon said, keeping his eyes fixed on Chick.

"What?" Chick said in disbelief.

"No fucking way," Stu snorted.

"Wanted to offer his assistance," Jadon said mocking Devon's British accent.

"With what?" Stu grumbled.

"All the legal shit that's going on. He said because we both care for Meg we should be able to form a truce to help her." Jadon tried to ignore the hint of truth that whispered ominously over Devon's words.

"That'd be all fine and dandy if he wasn't so fucking nuts," Chick said. "I don't trust him. And he is up to something. Where the hell did your dad go? Wasn't he looking in to this?"

"Yeah. But he said he needed to check out a lead. You know him. He doesn't like to mention what he's thinking unless he knows for sure." Jadon shook his head before letting out a constricted breath of frustration.

"He didn't even say where he was going?" Bob asked.

"Nope," Jadon said flatly.

"Meg know he called you?" Chick asked.

"Nope."

⇌

Stretching her left arm across her body, Meg slammed shut the door of Erin's Jeep. As she sat next to Erin, she rifled through the mail she'd just picked up from her box at the local post office. Quickly she scanned for anything that demanded her immediate attention.

"Oh, wonderful," Meg mumbled.

Looking over, Erin tried to read the return address on the envelope. "Who . . . ?"

"My attorney. God. I cringe whenever I see his name." Meg dug her thumb into the envelope, trying to dislodge the stack of papers folded inside. "Oh, goodie, in addition to this, he sent his bill. Odd how I can go weeks without any activity, except to receive a bill. Seems he never drops the ball on billing me."

"What is it?" Erin asked with a cringed face.

"Looks like this Strum idiot is really serious about taking me to court. His attorney wants to give me a deposition. They want to bring everything that has to do with the book into court."

"That sounds bad. What do they want?"

"All of my notes, computer records . . . everything to do with my novel." Letting the papers fall onto her lap, Meg looked up at the post office in disbelief. "Shouldn't my attorney have already requested the same thing from Strum?"

"Yeah. That would make sense."

"I'm getting so tired of telling this guy to do his job. Why can't he just *try* to fight for me? I'm innocent. That should mean something."

Letting her Jeep roll backward out of the parking lot, Erin slowly pulled onto the road and headed toward the studio.

"At least your checkup went well," Meg smiled, looking over at Erin.

"Yeah. I'm glad about that. Real glad. Thanks for coming with."

"Not a problem. I didn't have any plans. Between falling apart, putting myself back together, just to fall apart again . . . I really didn't have anything else to do," Meg said with a chuckle.

"Have you heard from Devon?"

Meg looked at Erin with surprise, "Yeah. Just this morning. He called."

"And you answered . . ."

Meg nodded. "I did. I don't know why."

"What did he say? If you don't mind my asking?"

"You can ask anything. You know that." Meg gave Erin a raised eyebrow before looking out the window to contemplate the conversation she had with Devon. "Oh . . . he . . . he wanted to make sure I was okay. He said if all the legal crap gets any worse, he fears it might damage my career, not to mention the book. It's all starting to overshadow the book already."

"Do you have any more press engagements?"

"No, except for one radio interview. It seems Devon was able to buy me some time after that debacle in New York. Except for this one interview, but its not a big deal. God, I feel so powerless, Erin," Meg said, noticing her last statement tapped into the natural spring of tears that perpetually flowed inside her heart.

"What can be done? Isn't your publishing company helping at all? I would think they would have to. It just sounds so bizarre that you've been left to flounder around on your own," Erin said, pulling into the alley in front of the studio.

"I don't know. I know Devon would know. God, Erin . . . ," Meg said, dropping her head forward. "A big part of me wants to just allow him to fix it. Fix it all. Then I could enjoy my life with Jadon."

Switching off the ignition, Erin tapped at the steering wheel lightly with her fingertips. "Do you think Devon was in your house?"

"Why would he be?" Meg looked at Erin with question. "I can't see him in there. Maybe I can't see him in there because my mind can't figure out why he would be in there. I don't know. I do know that I feel like I'm trapped in a web I can't get out of, and if Devon can snip the silky strings that are holding me here . . . I . . . I don't know. I just know I want to be rid of it."

"You would be rid of that, but in its place you would have Devon," Erin said, opening the door to the studio.

"Hey, there's the lovely ladies," Stu said with a smile.

"Hey, babe, what's the good word?" Chick said, wrapping his arms snuggly around Erin.

"I'm good. The baby is good. Weight is good, and growing right on schedule," Erin said holding Chick tight.

"Good. I didn't want to be forced to stop our potato chips and cheese binges," Chick said, giving Erin a kiss on the forehead.

"Ooh, chips and cheese. How come we ain't invited?" Stu asked.

"Because it's like at midnight when the craving hits," Chick said, turning around to face everyone. "I'm a regular in the Ralph's check out line around half past midnight."

"Not too late for me," Stu laughed.

"What's wrong?" Jadon said, looking at Meg.

"Nothing. Nothing new really," Meg answered taking a deep breath.

"We stopped by the post office after my appointment. Strum's lawyer wants to depose Meg and see all her files," Erin said, crossing her arms tightly across her chest.

"Christ," Bob said, looking at Stu in disbelief.

"I shouldn't have signed for that envelope," Meg said, trying to laugh it off.

"What the hell? A subpoena?" Jadon looked down at the papers Meg handed him.

"Yeah. They want everything to do with my book. It doesn't make sense though. Shouldn't my attorney have been the one who subpoenaed Strum?" Meg answered.

"I see we have another bill," Jadon said shaking his head.

"And this is the attorney our guy recommended?" Stu asked.

"Yeah. I'm not too fucking happy about that. I need to find out what the hell he was thinking. He said this guy was good," Chick said.

"Good at what?" Bob said.

"He's good at billing Meg," Stu said, lighting up another cigarette.

"Man, this is creeping up past $50,000, and I swear he hasn't done anything," Jadon said, running his finger down the list of itemized charges. "He spent four hours reading e-mails?"

"What?" Chick said. "Okay. He's gotta go."

"Who do we use?" Erin asked.

"Someone has to know someone. Anyone would be better than this deadbeat. He's just trying to make money off Meg. He knows she has money, so he is sitting on this, letting the fucking clock tick," Chick said, scrolling through his contact list on his cell phone.

"How long before the deposition?" Bob asked.

Hearing the door, Meg turned around quickly to watch Raffi and Flora walk in. Offering only a weak but sincere smile, Meg attempted to appear happy. Looking down at the floor, she pulled her right arm tight to her chest and tried to stretch the muscles in her neck.

"Oh, what's going on?" Raffi asked.

"Things are fucking boiling out of control, that's what's going on," Stu said, after letting a long ribbon of smoke escape his lips.

Sitting down on the arm of the sofa next to Stu and Bob, Flora listened to the latest news. She broke her gaze from the coffee table to intermittently look up at Raffi while the many voices that filled the room discussed their frustration with the attorney, their anxiety regarding the upcoming deposition, and the madness that accompanied the situation.

Walking up behind Flora, Raffi wrapped his finger through the long silver and black ringlets that flowed down from Flora's face. "What are you thinking?"

Squinting, Flora shook her head with hesitance. "I just don't see a hearing or a trial."

"Well, I hope not, but according to the attorney and the county of Los Angeles there's going to be not only a deposition, but a trial, and Meg's got to bring all sorts of shit to show Strum's lawyer," Chick said, keeping his eyes fixed on the papers in his hand.

Turning quickly to face Jadon, Flora started to speak, then closed her mouth, rethinking her words.

"What?" Jadon asked cautiously.

"Nothing. I just . . . Devon called someone this morning . . . ," Flora said.

"Me," Meg said.

"He called you?" Jadon asked in shock, looking at Meg.

"You were already heading to the studio and . . . you left the house with such optimism about my hand . . . I didn't want to spoil it. So I put off telling you. You've had so much on your mind."

"What happened to your hand?" Erin asked.

"She moved it," Jadon said turning to look at Erin then at the guys, noticing they were looking at him with disappointment for not having revealed that Devon had also called him that morning.

"What? That is great. You didn't tell me," Erin said.

"I didn't say anything because it hasn't moved since, and I'm not positive it ever did," Meg said, turning her attention back toward Jadon. "Maybe . . . this is a sign. Maybe the phone call . . ."

"Don't say it. God, please don't think it," Jadon said.

"I just want peace. And if this is how the Universe wants to play this one, I'll play. If it means getting beyond it so we can finally breathe and enjoy our lives together . . . ," Meg said. "Maybe this is his way of making up for what he did. His way of trying to fix the wrongs he did. And Christ . . . I need to feel like I get justice with this. That novel is about my mom. Her life, and the one she dreamed of having. And now when I think of it, all I think about is that horrible creature who is trying to say the story is his, and the self-righteous attorney that isn't helping me find justice."

Everyone turned silent from the realization that not only was the novel Meg wrote, about her claiming her voice as a writer, but more than anything, it was about Meg finding closure for her mother. Every line that Meg wrote setting her mother free also shadowed the reality of her mother's depression and discontentment. It was obvious to everyone that in many ways Meg was losing her mother all over again, only this time Fate disguised itself within the greed of others.

"I'm sorry, baby," Jadon said, holding Meg tight. "I'm so sorry. You need closure. You should have closure. And if you feel Devon is the one that can help . . ." He paused. "Do it."

~

The day had left a layer of heavy and exhausting film covering Jadon's body, but with his eyes forced open from the endless hum of thoughts that circled his mind, he turned to look at the clock, and noticed it was 3:33 a.m. Rolling his head back onto the pillow, he stared at the ceiling, then at Meg lying next to him.

Turning his body toward hers, he ran his hand slowly across her shoulder and down her arm. He'd do anything for her, of that there was no question. Nothing about Devon felt right, though; it felt wrong — not just wrong, it felt dangerous.

Running his fingers across her face, Jadon watched as she slowly opened her eyes. Pausing for a moment with her mouth held partially open in thought, Meg asked, "What if there is no God?"

Tilting his head gently to the side, Jadon looked at her with concern. "Where are your thoughts right now?"

"All over the place," she smiled sleepily. "My thoughts, they're like little kids right now. I'm trying to corral them into bed so I can finally go to sleep. But they won't go. They keep running around inside my head. And some of the more rambunctious kids keep screaming that all this belief I have in God and Fate . . . is silly. What if we're all just on our own, and there is nothing beautiful helping us out."

Resting his head next to Meg's on her pillow, Jadon searched her face with his eyes. "How do you explain this?" he whispered, pointing his finger back and forth between the two of them. "This is Fate. How else do you explain buying the house right next door to me? And the beautiful music you would play on your balcony. The music that brought me to my knees. And you, everything about you . . . every time I look at you, I feel complete."

"But now I can't make that same beautiful music. So . . . how is that part of Fate?"

"Maybe there is more to Fate than just the beautiful stuff. Maybe it's about taking us down certain roads so that we become who we are supposed to become. Hell if I know. But something about that makes sense to me, and it feels right. Just as right as it feels when you're lying next to me. You have this mind that is constantly going with thoughts that run around. Maybe you should look at it as if you're their teacher. And it's time that you tell those thoughts who's boss. Those troublemakers that are saying all that crap about God and Fate . . . put them in a timeout." Jadon stopped to give Meg a soft smile. "And the thoughts that are well behaved and make you feel good . . . spend some time with them. Play with them, give them a hug. I think they'll hug you back."

"You're really something. You know that?" Meg said, expressing the words through a warm smile.

"How do you come up with that stuff ? It's good. Next book I write . . . you're helping me."

Burying his head next to Meg's, Jadon let out a soft yawn before answering. "I'll be there."

Letting a few moments of silence fill the room, Meg whispered, "Promise to always be the first thing I see when I open my eyes."

"Promise."

Chapter 18

"We had to cruise," Chick said, closing the door to the studio once Erin hurried through. "How much time we got?"

Looking over his shoulder at the clock on the microwave, Jadon said, "You have plenty of time. Meg's interview doesn't start for another ten minutes."

"Should we tape this?" Bob asked, giving Stu a quick look.

"Do we even fuckin' know how to tape what's on the radio?" Stu questioned.

"That's okay. I don't know if she'd want to listen to it anyway. She wasn't in the best of moods today," Jadon said.

"Did you ask why?" Flora asked.

"Other than the obvious," Stu said.

"No. But when I walked into the bedroom she was sitting on the bed trying to get her hand to move again. She was frustrated that it wasn't. She knows I'm not lying. I saw her hand move. Hell, I saw her whole arm move when she threw that glass bird across the room."

"What did the therapist say?" Raffi asked.

"She thought it made sense, as there isn't a physical reason preventing Meg from using her hand," Jadon said.

"It's her mind," Stu said in a low grumble.

"What the fuck is worse? Jesus, I mean . . . when you think about it. How do you fight your own mind?" Chick said, handing Erin a bottle of water.

"Thanks, babe. Well, this interview is a good thing, though," Erin said.

"Yeah. She was told by Trish that this interview would calm the waves caused when she walked out on the conference in New York. Of course . . . ," Jadon paused. "She was also told if she botches this interview . . . they'd drop her."

"They can't do that. They got a contract," Stu said, raising his voice.

"Anyone can get out of a contract," Chick said, with a huff of disgust. "Our first record company sure seemed to find a way out of theirs."

"How do you feel about today?" Erin said, looking at Flora.

"Nervous. I just feel like something is about to happen."

⁓

After the legendary interviewer Mac McPherson pushed the hanging microphone in front of Meg's mouth and gave her a warm smile, she slid on the headphones and took a nervous swallow. This was her first radio interview since the conference in New York, and Meg was keenly aware that she was already becoming a writer known for controversy. The book-reading public was still spinning from the discovery that she was the author of such controversial books as *Unleashed*. And by walking off a stage in front of a roomful of reporters she had garnered the same publicity given to rock stars known for their off the wall antics, or worse, poor composure. All of which, Meg knew, were misguided labels. Regardless, the labels were repeatedly stuck under her picture and name over the last few weeks. Adding to the lead weight sitting in her stomach were the flat-toned words coming from Trish at Handle House Publishing Company that morning. *"If you want to be a rock star, do it on your own watch. We need a serious writer, both with pen and tongue."* Meg thought the harsh words were both unwarranted and just plain rude. It was obvious the media was putting a bad spin on her relationship with Jadon. *If only they knew, if only they cared. Jadon is one of the few things holding me together*, Meg said to herself. Although she always suspected it, now she knew with certainty that society doesn't care. Instead, once caught in the large, judgmental eye of the media, her life was just another meal consumed by the masses. And like a good meal, everything about her was chewed upon, savored for a second, then swallowed or spit out.

Mac McPherson again flashed a reassuring smile at Meg. A red light flashed on. They were on the air.

"Today we are privileged to have Meg Scott with us. And as many of you know, Ms. Scott for years . . . pumped out tome after tome under the name Kathleen Kelly. I must tell you, Meg, that sitting across the table from you is much like stumbling upon the Holy Grail. For years, your identity was kept secret. You must have had a very good publishing company to let you do that," Mac laughed, giving Meg a nod that she could offer up some commentary if she wanted.

"Uh . . . well, I guess they were good at discretion," Meg said, turning down the volume of her voice in her headphones.

"In the short time we have, can you share with us how you came up with your storylines. I mean . . . I'm a guy, obviously . . . ," Mac said in his warm baritone, "and yet I loved your books, even though every protagonist was a woman. Still . . . I loved that these women had such strong voices. They were dealt remarkable challenges, had the strength to overcome them, and charged ahead without crumbling."

"Ah . . . I guess, I always thought these women were a shade of myself. Not so much *the me* that occupies my every day. But a version, buried deep inside. I can't say I would be as strong as they were if I had to deal with the same issues they had, though."

"Phew . . . and they had 'em. One challenge after another. *Unleashed* made me believe that love doesn't have to fit into a mold. I liked that. I have to say Meg . . . the steam in that one easily peeled the wallpaper off the walls."

Meg laughed, recalling writing the love scenes in *Unleashed*. "Yes, that one . . . I had fun with that."

Returning his voice to its usual state of seriousness, Mac asked, "Do you think the movie did it justice?"

Knowing enough not to be honest, Meg answered, "I think it captured a great deal of the story. It was beautiful to watch."

"And there is word that *Wings to Fly*, the fictionalized story about your own mother, might be made into a movie . . ." Mac let his words linger so Meg would continue with the direction of what he was saying.

Meg nodded. "That's what I'm hearing as well," she laughed softly. "That would be hard to watch. For me . . . I mean."

"I would imagine, I would imagine. I lost my father when I was young. Photographs of him are hard to look at, even so many years later. Now . . . what do you say to those critics who say your books aren't . . . *real* literature."

"I don't say anything."

"I guess I should rephrase that. What do you think about that? Looking at some of these statements, there is a group . . . that feels *Unleashed* is immoral. Loving two men . . . having sex with two men at the same time, to be more to the point . . . is immoral. Then there is this faction that criticizes your appearance at the New York book fair. They say that walking off the stage showed the public, your audience, that you simply don't care. Writing is about more than throwing words together, you have to be able to talk about more than just storylines. On one end of the spectrum you have people who want to give your work an award, such as with *Wings to Fly*. Then on the other end, you have people that want to challenge your right to free speech. And as is usually the case with critics, some have gotten pretty nasty."

"Yes, they seem to feel it's acceptable to be nasty while criticizing me for being what they consider to be nasty," Meg chuckled at the obvious hypocrisy. "I think if people like my work, well . . . that feels good. It feels good when one's work is appreciated and enjoyed. If they don't . . . well, that's okay, too. But when it comes to being judged, I simply have chosen not to care what they think. I can't. I have to internally just say, fuck it."

"Whoa," Mac said startled. "This is daytime, Meg."

Meg cringed. She knew that dropping the forbidden *f* bomb was a broadcasting no-no. Yet, it slipped out. It symbolized how she felt; no other words said it as honestly as those two words.

"Sorry," Meg said. "It's just a word."

"True. Yet… it's not a pretty word."

"Life isn't pretty," Meg countered.

"True again. Yet we have so many words to choose from, some less vulgar than others."

"I don't find that word to be vulgar. I think more attention needs to be paid to intent and word meaning. A word is simply just letters combined into an audible sound, one that has a designated meaning. Or, such as with this word, multiple meanings." Meg kept her voice calm and low. "I'm sorry I said it and caused you any offense, or offense to any of your listeners."

"Obviously you don't feel everyone and anyone should be tossing that word around. You wouldn't want kids using it," Mac said raising an eyebrow, pleased he came up with the angle he did.

"I don't have any children. But if I ever were to be so blessed as to have them . . . I would put more focus and emphasis on how the word is used. I would caution them more to refrain from using words that hold at their core a meaning of hate and racism. Those, in my opinion, are vulgar words."

⁂

It had been hours after nightfall had darkened the room. And with her gaze focused on the wall in front of her, Meg's only movements were the one's her hand involuntarily made while holding the phone hard against her ear, while she sat on the side of her bed.

Ending the call, Meg stared at the phone. Her silent pause and inability to move was caused not by the late hour but by the words Trish at Handle House had just spoken. Setting the phone back in its cradle next to her bed, she closed her eyes and leaned her head back. The day felt long. After her interview with Mac McPherson, Meg knew in her bones something was going to happen. But unlike the nervous excitement one feels knowing they are about to receive a surprise gift, this nervousness made her heart skip with anxiety and dread. In a failed attempt to outrun and outsmart the doom she feared was making its way toward her, Meg tried to sprint through her day, keeping herself busy until she finally collapsed from exhaustion. Moments after her head hit the pillow, the phone rang.

"They are . . . ," Meg paused to collect herself while turning on the bed to look at Jadon. "They are severing my contract."

"What? Why?" Jadon said, stunned.

"Um . . . they feel that despite their initial thoughts, they realize now, that I am too much of a gamble, and that I do not fit well within the demographic they wanted for me."

"But . . . your demographic is . . . women like you. So how could *you* not be a good fit? That doesn't make sense."

Meg nodded quietly. Nothing made sense anymore. But in many ways this new turn of events did make sense. It made perfect sense. It matched all the mind-boggling things doled out over the past few months. And within that rather large bag of heartache, being without a publisher for the first time in her writing career seemed almost fitting.

"The people who bought your books when you wrote under Kathleen Kelly wanted characters who were strong, Meg. That's even what that McPherson guy said. Yet . . ." Jadon stopped, realizing he didn't have the words to describe his confusion and disappointment.

"They feel my opinions are not those held by my demographic. It doesn't really make sense to me either.

Trish said that they are a respectable publishing house, and that my use of profanity on a radio program airing in the early afternoon showed that I do not respect them, or those within my demographic," Meg said, sliding under the covers and pulling the sheets up slowly around her shoulders.

"I don't believe that. The women . . . the people that buy your books . . . want real people, in real situations, who have the mind and willpower to overcome whatever is thrown at them. And I think what you said was awesome," Jadon said, flashing a proud smile.

Looking at Jadon's bright face, Meg couldn't help but smile in return. "If only you were my publishing company. You're a rock star. Rock stars are allowed a colorful vocabulary. I am a writer; I'm supposed to know better. Remind me to dig out my thesaurus tomorrow. I need to find alternate words for fuck it."

"I think the writer is the one who's supposed to have the colorful vocabulary."

"Maybe within the pages of the books they write, but it is apparent they don't want me to have such a vivid vocabulary when speaking in public."

"Now what? I mean, what happens next?" Jadon asked, wrapping his arm across Meg and pulling her tightly beside him.

Meg didn't answer. She had the words to voice what she was thinking, but she didn't want to see the look of sadness created once those words reached Jadon's ears.

"I know what you're thinking," Jadon said, lifting his head to look Meg in the eye.

"I can't help but think it. Try to tell me that everything isn't pointing me in that direction."

"That's exactly why I think it's the wrong direction."

"Or maybe it's the right direction. I've asked God for help. I've asked for the divine heavens to give me some help with all this crap. And this is what happens."

Chasing Nirvana

Chapter 19

"What do you mean he thinks someone is following him?" Devon said, enunciating his words slowly and purposefully into the phone.

Tapping the tip of his long silver pen against his mouth, Devon listened patiently while Blake gave him the latest update and problematic situation beginning to simmer with George Strum. During intermittent intervals, he looked mindfully off into the distance while trying to make sense of the sudden reluctance Strum was expressing regarding the upcoming deposition and court appearance.

"Why does he feel this person is a threat? Can he even describe this person who's supposedly lurking in the shadows?" Devon asked skeptically.

Although he had never met George Strum, Devon knew enough about him to confidently assume Strum's mind was not a fortress of aptitude or fortitude. But like many, Strum was easily enticed by the lifestyle money could afford. Once the fictional scenario was placed before him that his claim was an easy win, and one that would provide him with millions, there was no easier puppet than George. Until now.

With his pen held motionless in front of him, Devon felt his stomach turn slowly. Taking a long purposeful breath, he held his poise while Blake relayed Mr. Strum's description of the man he had seen too often as of late.

"How tall?" Devon asked.

Closing his eyes, the picture slowly painted itself within his mind. What he didn't like was that the newly created image mirrored perfectly the image of the man who was oddly out of place at the hotel in New York during the recent book fair. From the moment Devon saw him, he knew he had brushed shoulders with him. As of yet, he still couldn't remember where. Regardless of his memory's inability to bring the information to light, he knew with certainty he had shared space with the man before. Instantly upon seeing him in New York, Devon knew the man was there with a purpose: a purpose that had something to do with him.

"Oh, no. I heard you correctly," Devon said, attempting to explain his silence. "I was just going over what you said in my mind. Sounds like quite an imposing fellow. Mr. Strum lives up in the mountains; I would have to believe the mountains harbor many a large man. I'm not exactly positive I understand why this one should stand out."

Taking slow, deep breaths to prevent his body from succumbing to the uneasiness that was already taking hold of his mind, Devon fell silent once again while Blake explained all that George had recently shared that morning while speaking with him.

From what Devon could gather, this large, commanding figure was showing up almost everywhere George was. And although this figure seemed always preoccupied, George couldn't help but feel as though his every move was being monitored.

"Did Strum talk to him?" Devon asked. Hearing the answer, he continued, "Of course. Not surprising. Strum is frightened of his own shadow; of course he would be frightened of this man. Strum is only five-six . . . five-seven wearing trainers," he said with a laugh, but no smile. "What in blazes does he want you to do about it? You're his attorney, not his bodyguard."

After allowing Blake to answer, Devon shook his head. "That's not an option. He has to continue on. I don't care if he feels the man is silently hostile. Frankly, I don't even know what that means. Either he has threatened Strum or not. Think up something. Some added incentive. Add something to the pot of gold he believes he'll be getting. He can't see past his greed."

Hanging up the phone, Devon spun around in his chair to face the living room in his hotel suite. If Strum was as pathetic as he believed him to be, there was a good chance he didn't have the resolve to finish the race and satisfy his own thirst for money regardless of the prize being waved at the end of the line.

Spinning back around, Devon smiled as he read the number displayed on his cell phone.

"Hello, Devon," Meg said, holding her front door open, allowing him to walk inside.

"I have to say, your call was rather unexpected, Meg," Devon smoothly lied, while sliding his hands into the deep pockets of his black trousers as he walked casually through the living room, and looked out the balcony. "But always welcomed," he said, turning to give Meg a friendly grin.

"Well, I really didn't know who else to call."

"I hope I was your first choice," Devon let out a laugh. "Not your only choice."

"Oh. Of course. I guess I didn't know anyone else who even *could* help me. It seems things are such a mess, they require skill. Not everyone has that," Meg said, lowering herself onto the large white chair in her living room.

Casually taking a seat on the sofa, Devon crossed his legs while watching Meg's every move.

"How are you doing?" he asked. "I'm not too concerned with the *mess*. I trust I will be able to clean it up. But how are you?"

"I can't tell the difference between where I stop and where the mess begins. So, I don't know how I am."

Allowing his head to give a deep, thoughtful nod, Devon smiled softly. "I guess we need to fix that. What has happened that is such a problem?" he asked, raising his right eyebrow while running his hand over his knee, smoothing out the invisible wrinkles.

"I don't have a publisher anymore. That's what's happened."

"Ah. I see," Devon said. "That's a slight problem. But fixable. Next."

"I'm told I don't measure up to the expectations of my own demographic," Meg said, letting the words gently reveal her bitterness.

"That's nonsense." Devon showed only calm ease.

"To me it is, and maybe to you . . . " Meg's voice began to elevate.

Motioning with his hand for Meg to relax, Devon said softly, "Trust me. It's nonsense. It is obvious I won't recommend that publishing house ever again, as they do not know what they are talking about. Is there more?"

"I guess I'm a gamble, and most likely, due to showing signs of being unmanageable . . . promoting my book will be increasingly more difficult. I . . . swore during a radio interview . . . ," Meg said, fluttering her hand in the air.

Wincing slightly, Devon's face continued to hold its grin. "I heard it. I happen to think the interview was quite good. I liked what you said."

"Trish didn't."

"All right," Devon paused, while running his finger across his bottom lip. "I've been considering something, and I think this is a sign that my idea is coming to fruition and indeed falling into place. I've had the idea of beginning a specialized division of Hathaway Publishing. One that is . . . edgier, for a lack of a better word. By that, I don't mean just the writing we publish, but the authors as well. I want to see writers who have minds, and speak them. People want that, I feel certain. I want to buy up the rights and put

Wings to Fly under this new division of Hathaway Publishing. You would, of course, need to work hard to honor the publicity engagements," he said, giving Meg a quick look of authority.

"I can do that. I know I can," Meg said, sitting up straighter. "I can. I just want to be me. I don't want someone coming after my friends though."

Devon cocked his head to the side, "I can't promise what someone will or will not ask or say. However, if you don't like what is being asked, I imagine you can just tell them to fuck off," he said with a large smile.

Meg laughed to herself. She liked what she was being told. She liked the sound of it. It felt right. At the moment it didn't even bother her that Devon was the one saying it. All of his words felt like a life preserver being tossed out into the turbulent ocean. More than anything it felt good to have something to hold on to, and to feel the tug of a competent, powerful hand pulling her to safety.

"Meg . . . ," Devon said, interrupting her moment to absorb the new information. "I will . . .try to keep our time together to a minimum. Out of . . . respect. But we will need to interact. I hope that won't be an issue. I don't want this new beginning, one that very well might remove a great deal of your current stress, to inadvertently bring new stress."

"We've talked about this, this decision to call you," Meg said, not feeling comfortable discussing Jadon with Devon.

"And Jadon . . . ," Devon said, motioning for Meg to reveal a bit more than she had.

"He agrees. Something has to change. He knows and understands the position I'm in. He wants me to be able to enjoy my life, not just be a prisoner to the insanity that has been hovering around as of late. He's good," Meg said, knowing that Devon was paying too close attention to her words.

She didn't say Jadon liked the idea, or wanted her to ask for help from Devon. Jadon agreed things were beyond what they were capable of handling alone, yet he still felt that almost any other option would be better than calling Devon. Meg could tell that Jadon, after hearing her out, didn't want to try to sway her. Jadon's feelings were based on his gut and his heart.

But he knew, and Meg knew, his gut and heart didn't have the wherewithal to fix the mess that surrounded them. If they did, the mess would have been gone shortly after it arrived. Instead, Meg was all too aware of how time had stopped like a clock that's lost power. Until fixed, the clock sits in a locked position.

Meg couldn't say she liked her decision to call Devon. But there were so many things she didn't like as of late, it hardly mattered. If the forces of the Universe were leaving her with no choice except Devon, then maybe good would ultimately come from it. Starting up with someone new felt overwhelming — not to mention the work involved in finding someone new. Time and money spent just to discover all of their shortcomings and problems. Devon she knew: the good and the bad.

"I tried to offer my assistance. I . . . ," Devon said, shaking his head to show how absurd his actions had been. "I called Jadon directly. I knew it wouldn't be an easy call. But Meg . . . I wanted to let him know that if we could somehow put our feelings aside, put the past behind us, we might be able to get you back on track."

Meg stared at Devon. "When did you call him?" she asked, trying to hide how startled she was.

Finding it a struggle to hold down the smile that unexpectedly emerged on his face, Devon quickly reshaped it into a purposeful frown. "Oh, let's see . . . yesterday. I reached out to both of you. One right after the other. Perhaps I'm so dreadful you both don't even want to utter my name to one another," he said, enjoying the revelation that Jadon hadn't told Meg of their discussion.

"No. It's not like that," Meg said, standing up to walk to the balcony. "We just get busy."

Knowing that his plans were being primed by a most unexpected source, Devon weighed his words and actions carefully.

"Well, I have to be going. I hope you find some relief knowing that I will take care of everything," Devon said, pushing himself up from the chair and walking onto the balcony next to Meg. "Oh . . . I will have someone set up your Twitter and Facebook pages. No sense muddling through yourself when there are people so well versed in all that technical web gadgetry."

Turning to face Devon, Meg said unexpectedly, "Why did you come to Bay City the night of the book fair? You flew out that night, correct? I hope you don't mind me asking, but . . . why?"

Not removing his gaze from the ocean that moved beyond the balcony rail, Devon showed no signs of hesitance in answering. "I had to meet with a medical specialist in Lost Angeles the next morning. I wanted to spend the evening in flight, allowing more time to prepare once I landed."

"Oh," Meg stammered, "Are . . . you . . . all right?"

"Nothing life threatening, much to your friends' heartbreak, I'm sure." He turned to give Meg a tender grin. "But to me it feels a bit like death," Devon said, biting his lower lip to show his words required a physical distraction to prevent their emotional impact.

"I don't understand," Meg said.

Looking down thoughtfully at Meg, Devon kept his voice light with intentional sadness, knowing the words he'd carefully constructed and was about to share, although false, were painful enough in their origin to form an unshakable bond between them. "Unlike you dear, I may have the use of both my hands . . . but, it seems something, call it God or Fate or what have you, has decided to be a bit cruel to me as well. You see Meg . . . unless my brother chooses to have children, the Hathaway name ends with me."

Chapter 20

It wasn't just a matter of how reclusive George Strum had suddenly become that had John bothered; he didn't like the way his stomach was swirling with nervous energy — a vortex of energy that made no sense considering everything in Shaver Lake, California, was low-key and peaceful. His internal energy didn't fit what life was presenting him with. Unless of course, it was a harbinger of things to come.

But no one, not even Jadon, knew where he was. And it was apparent to John that George offered no real threat. John wasn't watching him because he was dangerous. He was watching him to unearth the person who was. Any seasoned detective can tell the difference between the puppet and the puppeteer.

Motioning for a refill of coffee, John looked out the window of the small diner that sat in the hub of town and watched as cars slowly moved by. Keeping an eye on traffic wasn't his priority, however; keeping an eye on the post office sitting across from the diner was. George's trips to the post office were as consistent as nightfall.

Rubbing the skin under his chin, John contemplated his next steps. Days of watching George Strum had provided him with close to no information. Most of what he learned — information proving his theories correct that someone was using Strum as their obedient puppy — he learned from countless hours online digging into Strum's background, peering through windows while Strum made his daily post office trip, not to mention digging through his trash.

The one piece of knowledge sitting in bright contrast to Strum's claims was the fact that his own mother had, in reality, lived a very fulfilled life, one that allowed her to enjoy the sun drenched beaches of Australia and southern Europe, as well as the mountains of Scandinavia. She had been successful, and although a widow at the time of her own death, her time while married seemed full of love. John wasn't the most philosophical person, but from what he could tell, there would be no cause for George to feel compelled to write a heartfelt story giving his mother the life she dreamed when she had apparently already lived it.

❦

With her left hand pecking across the keyboard, Meg typed slowly.

Just as surely as she knew her own thoughts, Amanda knew she wasn't ever going back. There would be no regrets, there would be no steps retraced. She'd spent the last ten years of her life contemplating this moment, but only now had she found the courage to manifest her contemplations. Or was it courage that found her? Either way, she knew she would never turn around.

Thinking about it now, those years of thought and contemplation were wasted. Life she would never be able to recapture. And yet it took each and every one of those years to create the person she needed to become. Her mind was already strong. But only now was her spirit as strong as her right arm, the arm that brought down her husband with one quick blow to the back of the head with a cast iron skillet.

Harnessing her ragged breaths, Amanda tried not to focus on the last hour of her life; instead, she kept her eyes held steady on the dirt road that steadily unfurled beneath her feet like a long, dark ribbon.

Staring at the screen on her laptop, Meg took a deep breath. She hadn't planned on ever writing again. But in the calm weeks that now surrounded and cushioned her, something inside wanted to get out. Once again, her swirling thoughts and frustrated soul needed release. Looking at the clock, Meg chuckled at the time it took for her left hand to peck out three paragraphs. At the sound of the doorbell, she easily shifted her thoughts from self-criticism to excitement.

"Hey! Hey, Larry," Erin said, bending down to give Big Larry a rub on the head before walking inside. "You look kind of tired, Meg. You okay?"

"Oh, yeah. I was… well, I was writing. Took forever to pound out a few paragraphs, but . . . ," Meg said, letting her words trail off while her head bounced back and forth with uncertainty.

"I think that's great. It doesn't surprise me."

"That makes one of us," Meg smiled, running her hand across the soft cushions that covered the lounge chairs on her balcony, ensuring they were dry. A habit formed from years spent on the east coast.

"Think about it. You've logged . . . what . . . three weeks of virtually no problems. As you would say, you're no longer wrapped under the suffocating blanket of insanity and crap," Erin laughed, trying to impersonate Meg.

Meg threw herself onto the chair and shook her head with amazement. "I know. It's been heaven. In one quick move, Devon pried that parasitic lawyer off of me and has a legion of lawyers that are actually interested in doing their jobs, which is winning my case."

"Speaking of . . . you haven't mentioned Devon a lot lately. I mean, I was out of town at my folk's house, but even in our e-mails you haven't really mentioned him. I have to wonder a little."

"Erin . . . he has been great. He's been keeping his distance. I don't know if he's just busy, or if he's doing it intentionally. Either way, other than just phone calls, it's been very, very quiet. I meet with him tomorrow. But that will be only the second time I've met with him since he took this mess on."

"It wasn't a mess for him, it seems. I see while I was gone your book reached the number one spot on the New York Times Bestseller list. Congrats, Meg. You and your mom deserve it," Erin said, leaning over to tighten her hand around Meg's.

"Finally. God. Ha," Meg laughed, letting out a sigh that emptied her chest.

"And our man Jay ... he is doing well with the whole Devon thing . . . ?" Erin waved her hand lightly in front of her.

"There really isn't anything for him not to be doing well with. It's going so smooth. It's all falling into place. There isn't anything not to enjoy. We spend our days just simply enjoying each other. No threats, no sickening attorneys. I'm finally able to focus on my book, and the upcoming interviews. It's good. It's very good. And how is the little Chick doing?"

Erin smiled while leaning her head back on the thick black cushion covering her chair. "Little Chick is doing very well," she said, patting her belly. "My blood pressure is coming under control. Thank God. I guess I need to eat a bit more, but other than that . . . things are right on schedule."

"Well. hell, isn't that a problem most every woman in world would like to have?" Meg laughed, handing Erin a glass of cucumber water.

"Oh, thank you. That first trimester hit me hard."

"What ever happened with Chick calling his mom?" Meg asked, stretching her legs out onto her lounge chair.

Erin shook her head sadly. "Oh, he isn't going to call her. And I'm not going to make him. The issue sitting between those two is big, deep and dark. It's especially sad because I know Chick would love to tell her about the baby. But he knows from too much experience that Lavinia will take the sunshine of this good news and turn it into rain. Her words have always left a dent in Chick's mind. Moms have that ability. Maybe both parents do. I don't know. Things she has said to him when he was in kindergarten he still remembers vividly to this day."

"Crazy how for all those months I never had a clue. I got so caught up in my own world."

"It's not like he ever offers to talk about it. He doesn't want to. He has come to a point where he knows there will never be a resolution. There is no happy ending to their story. So he simply, but painfully, moved on. To him, she's as good as dead. I know that sounds bad. But I think the only way he could get closure was to convince himself that for all intents and purposes his mother was and is dead."

"So many people have unfathomably messed up childhoods," Meg said with a laugh of sadness. "Take Jadon for example."

"Yeah. Speaking of which, where is John?" Erin asked, setting her glass on the small table sitting between the two lounge chairs.

"I guess he was off doing some investigation work then had to stop back at his house up in the mountains for a while. I'm not sure what is going on with that deal. Jadon doesn't really know either. All that screwy business about John thinking Devon was up to something. And now it turns out Devon is the only one able to help with this mess. Make sense of that."

"What does John think of Devon helping you, and his new publishing division taking over your book? He had to have had something to say about that, I would think."

"Jadon said his dad basically told him that nothing good will come of it," Meg said flatly, giving Erin a look of confusion. "And yet, only good has come from it."

⋘

Devon ran his finger across the cool stainless steel surface of his Walther PPK pistol with slow, purposeful movements; movements that matched his slow meditative thoughts. From the moment he was given the gun, he knew it had a destined purpose. Rubbing his fingertip over the rough black surface of the handgrip, he felt no sadness, no doubt or remorse, only the steady energy that surrounds the need to complete a long drawn out, all-consuming mission. Removing Jadon from Meg's life provoked in him the same level of emotion as taking out the over-filled trash can after a very tiring social gathering. A bothersome task, nothing he looked forward to doing, yet something he looked forward to having done, over and out of the way.

Picking up the pistol from the desk, Devon let his eyes float slowly over the dark blue steel barrel while reclining peacefully into the plush leather chair that moved in unison with his body. He then picked up the long, cylindrical silencer and carefully connected it to the barrel of the pistol, methodically twirling the silencer until it was screwed tightly into place. Extending his arm toward the window, Devon cast his eye over the barrel of the gun and whispered, "Goodbye."

There was no better place to find one's own mind than in the mountains, or so it seemed to John. He hadn't planned on ever coming back to his small cabin, but he needed a moment to make sense of the thoughts streaming through his mind.

Letting his focus drift to the birds swooping over Larry's head as the portly bulldog sniffed the hillside just beyond the deck, John shook his head with confusion; his body was trying to tell him something. From head to toe, he felt sick. Adding to the instinctual sickness he felt was the knowledge that unless he figured it out, something very terrible was going to happen. He pushed his foot lightly against the wood floor of his deck and rocked rhythmically back and forth in his rocking chair. As his body moved to the steady motion, he closed his eyes and let his thoughts do the same. Smiling, he thought of Emily. When he wanted to feel peace inside his soul, he always thought of her.

Chuckling softly, John remembered how Emily always could *feel* if something was about to happen, good or bad. His eyes began to water as he contemplated that maybe Emily was trying to send him a message.

"Ah . . . if you're trying to talk to me, Em, hell if I know what you're trying to say," he whispered. "Devon's up to somethin', Em. I know it, and you know it."

John opened his eyes and looked down at Lil' Larry, who was sitting patiently at his feet. As if in a daze, he stared at the large face of his bulldog, until Larry started to moan.

"Whatcha' need, Lar? You want up here?" John said in a sweetened tone, motioning to the log bench sitting next to his rocking chair. "You need up here, big guy? All right . . ."

John hoisted the hefty body of his bulldog onto the bench. Turning to look back over the mountain hillside, John tapped lightly at his shirt pocket without thought, his body responding to habitual movements; motored by autopilot, not deliberate contemplation. Startled by the empty discovery, he walked steadily toward his truck while his thoughts were preoccupied with Devon.

Why the hell did I leave my phone in here? John asked himself as he slid his hand across the seat toward his cell phone. Stopping quick, John's mind shifted. Choosing not to reach for his cell phone, he opened the glove compartment and pulled out his flask of whiskey. Taking a long drink, he wiped his mouth, and screwed the stainless steel cap back on. Letting the whiskey numb the rough edges of his mind, he grabbed his cell phone and flask, and walked back to the cabin.

"Anything happen while I was gone?" John said, sliding his body next to Larry's on the bench.

Looking over the mountain side, he let his mind go to the deep, winding places discovered only through liquor. Nothing good was ever found there. Yet, John could never satisfy his need to travel to those places. Within his heavy mind, observations and conclusions were found and made. None showed the beauty of the world, only the irony that proved that God was not a friendly fellow. To John, God was no more than a mere observer, just like he was. Every time he'd called out to God, he was met with silence. After years of praying, he stopped, concluding that either God was mute or John was deaf. Or worse, that he was a fool to have believed such a being even existed.

Taking another long sip of whiskey, John looked at his reflection on the side of the stainless steel flask. Not liking what he saw, he took another drink.

Sighing deeply, he shook his head. He'd reached a dead end. *Such is life*, he thought to himself, *such is life*. Rubbing his hand over Larry's head, he remembered how Emily could see the good in all things. She saw the bad, but she could look beyond it. He remembered the peaceful look in her eyes right before she died. He closed his own eyes and listened as the final words Emily spoke floated across his mind like a soft, painful song: *Take care of Jadon. Take care of him, John. He's not tough like you . . . he's like me. He sees the world through my eyes.*

With a clumsy hand, John wiped the tears from his cheeks. "Every time he looks at me, Em, I see you looking at me. Stops me dead in my tracks. Every time. I couldn't save you, Em, and it looks like I can't save him. I'm tapped out. If there is a God, tell him I need a bit of help down here."

Leaning his head back against the rounded logs of his cabin, John closed his eyes again, and felt the release of sleep.

Startled by the sound of his flask falling hard against the deck floor, John jumped. Wiping his hand over his face, he swallowed hard and noticed everything he had recently poured into his body was about to reappear. With wide steps, he shot off the deck and moved his large frame next to the nearest tree. Leaning against it, his body forcefully removed the whiskey from his body. Resting his head against his arm, John tried to gather his strength while the large tree patiently held him firmly balanced and in place.

"Christ," John said, looking around, trying to make sense of what had just happened.

Walking slowly toward his cabin, he quickened his pace once he heard his cell phone ringing.

"Yeah," John answered, still shaken by his sudden and violent stomach upset.

"Dad," Jadon said.

Hearing Jadon's voice, John's tone instantly softened. "What's wrong, son?

"Are, ah . . . are you coming back soon?"

John paused. Since his mother's death, Jadon had never once asked for him, making the words he was hearing hit hard against his heart. "Is everything okay?"

"Yeah. But I keep getting this feeling that it's just an illusion. I don't know. I just, I just was wondering if you could come back," Jadon said, swallowing hard.

"I'm on my way."

⇜

While the exhaustion of having successfully completed another day settled over him, Jadon reached down and grabbed the blanket covering Meg's bed and carefully pulled it over the two of them.

Looking up, Meg let her eyes relax on the image of Jadon as he covered both of them. Shrouded by the darkness offered by the late hour, she felt her heart tighten as it often did when she watched him. She knew from the first moment she met him that he owned her heart and always would. She watched as his long blonde hair swayed around his face while he made himself comfortable beside her. Second only to the beauty of his heart and mind were his eyes. Looking deeply into them, she felt her soul reconnect with the world that lives beyond this one. And she needed to see that world as often as possible. Within his eyes she found the hope that there was something bigger watching out for them.

"You're not going to forget about me tomorrow, are you?" Jadon smiled, pulling the pillow away from Meg's face.

"How could I?" She grinned, and happily changed the subject. "You know, you're really good at doing this stuff . . . ," Meg giggled, referring to what they had been doing for the last hour.

"Oh, yeah?" Jadon said, sliding his body tightly against hers. "You think so?" He ran his lips across Meg's cheek. Stopping with his mouth on hers, he lightly brushed his lips back and forth before pressing them hard against hers.

With eyes closed, Meg nodded. "Yes. You are very skilled. I don't want to know how you acquired such skill, but I can safely say you are indeed skilled."

"I think it has something to do with the person I'm with."

"Oh, that's a good save. Very good."

"It's the truth," he said, sliding his body on top of hers.

Running his fingers across Meg's face, he looked into her eyes, and sighed softly. Tomorrow Meg was meeting with Devon and everything inside of him told him it was the beginning of the end.

"I'll be okay tomorrow," she said.

"I know. Don't be fooled by him, Meg. Promise me. Keep him at a distance."

"I will. But you have to admit, things feel good now. Smooth. My book is finally thriving for the right reasons. He put an end to the legal crap. No subpoena, no deposition, no trial. And I am so, so relieved."

"I know. That's what worries me. I feel like he's just been waiting for the chance to rescue you." Jadon lowered his forehead onto hers.

"When is John coming back?" Meg asked softly, wanting an excuse to change the subject.

"Soon. I called him earlier today."

"Did you know your dad is a gifted writer?"

"Writer?"

"I went over to your place earlier, after I took Big Larry for a walk. And, well . . . I wasn't trying to snoop. I wasn't," Meg said sheepishly. "Well, maybe a little. I wanted to snoop a little. He had left some of his things, and he is so mysterious. I sort of looked through stuff . . ."

Lifting his head off of hers, Jadon stared at Meg intently. "And . . ."

"And . . . I found what looked like a poem, in with a lot of other things he wrote. I took it."

Sliding out from under Jadon, Meg pulled open the drawer next to the bed and fumbled through her papers.

"I buried it in here. I don't know why," Meg said in a hurried tone. "I guess, he sort of scares me, and you know . . . it's his, not mine, and I just took it. I better put it back if he's coming home soon. But . . ." She paused, looking at Jadon who was now sitting up in the bed staring intently at her. "I just think there's a side to your dad you really don't know. I think . . . this poem might shed some light on some of the hurt you've been dealing with all this time."

Feeling a wave of nervous energy wash over him, Jadon slid the sheet of paper from Meg's outstretched hand. Glancing down at his dad's hand writing, he slowly read the words.

Blood pours from the heart, forming endless streams
Deep waters of broken dreams
My heart cries out from the barren space, within his eyes I see your face
Don't you remember, we were going to die together
Never afraid to face the day, you promised your hand in mind
Painful vision to behold; the truth behind my distance untold
Love has two faces, one warm, one cold
Beauty isn't innocent nor is it kind; I was yours, and you were mine
But now you're gone, and I'm left walking an unsteady line
Love heals the heart just to wound it again

Not through words whispered in hurt, but from your absent eyes
We were going to die together
We were going to die together
Em

"Em . . . Mom. He wrote this to my mom," Jadon said softly, keeping his eyes held on the paper.

Meg curled her body next to his and wrapped her arm around him. "I think he's talking about your eyes," she said, pointing at the second line John had written.

"My . . . ," Jadon whispered.

Jumping off the bed, Meg walked quickly into the living room, and returned with the framed picture of Jadon's mom held in her hand. Curling her body behind his again, she held the picture in front of him.

"Your eyes. They are exactly like your mom's."

As he held the picture, Jadon stared at his mother. Smiling, he said, "Yeah . . . we were always told that. Everyone said it. I guess . . . I was so used to it, I kind of forgot. That and . . ." He stopped to wipe the tears from his eyes, while he looked closely at his mother's face. "After she died, I had to stop seeing it. I couldn't look in the mirror otherwise."

Running her hand through his hair, Meg said softly, "I can't imagine how hard that must have been. For both of you. And after reading this . . . it's like we've been given the chance to look directly into your dad's heart. I think he loves you deeply. I know it. Something happened that day when you fell in the well, but . . . I don't think it was for the reason you thought."

Looking up at Meg, Jadon gave her a soft kiss. "Tomorrow . . . while you're with the devil . . . " He smiled. "I mean Devon . . . I'm going to show this to Chick. I want to hear it surrounded by music. I can hear the melody already. Thank you."

Putting the picture and the poem next to their bed, Jadon turned and looked at Meg, who was already nestled under the comforter waiting for him.

"I don't know why I didn't tell you this before. Sometimes, I think I'm doing the right thing, and then later I realize it wasn't even close to being the right thing." Turning off the light, Jadon slid under the comforter next to Meg. "That day, a month ago, when

Devon called you out of the blue, he called me, too." As he looked up at the ceiling, he rubbed his hand over his face. "And when Flora asked who Devon called, you were honest. I wasn't. I don't know why. I've been struggling with it ever since. It's stupid. Because I still don't know fully why I didn't want you to know. But part of me didn't. Part of me didn't want you to know he was trying to sell me his idea of working together to help you. Maybe . . . I think it's because I've been afraid I might be wrong. And I'm just being stubborn. And that stubbornness has only added to your pain."

Pushing herself up on her left arm, Meg tilted her head softly to the side, allowing her long auburn hair to fall gracefully over her bare shoulder.

"Why are you smiling? What I did was bad. And I feel bad for it."

"I know he called you. Devon told me."

"And you never said anything?" Jadon questioned, holding his hand over his forehead.

"I was hoping you would. And you did."

Chasing Nirvana

Chapter 21

"It's never a good sign when the entire band is in the studio before noon. Means we're either getting old or getting square." Chick laughed, closing the door of the studio. "Especially you, Stu . . . you don't roll out of bed early for anyone."

"I slept like a fucking rock until 4:00 a.m., then, boom, I was wide awake. I heard this fucking horn. Sounded like an air horn. I looked out every window, but didn't see anything," Stu said, lighting a cigarette and tossing the lighter across the table to Bob. "Of course it was dark, but still. And I wasn't dreaming either. Weirdest Goddamn thing."

"I didn't sleep good, period," Bob said, stretching his neck.

"What's that?" Chick asked, looking at the paper Jadon had in his lap.

"This is part of the reason I showed up so early, that and . . . ," Jadon started to say.

"That and a little thing like the fact that there's a slick as shit demon over at his house, sitting on his sofa right now . . . ," Stu interrupted with a groan.

"Oh, yeah. That's right," Chick said, rubbing his hand across his forehead in frustration.

"What do you think of this?" Jadon asked, sliding the piece of paper over to Chick.

Mumbling the words under his breath as he read them, Chick quickly made his way through the poem before reading over it a second time.

"This hurts the ol' heart. You write this?" Chick said snapping his gum, looking at Jadon.

"No. My dad wrote it."

"No fucking way," Chick said in disbelief.

"Our words exactly," Bob said. "Let's put it to music."

"Yeah. We want to do something with it," Stu said, burying his body deeper into the plush sofa next to Big Larry.

"Where'd you find it?" Chick asked. "He didn't give it to you . . ."

"Meg did. She was at my place yesterday and said she saw some of his things there, and . . . she said she couldn't help herself. She nosed through his things and stumbled across it. It blew her away," Jadon said, taking a long drag on his cigarette before crushing it in the ashtray.

"He's talking about how much you look like your mom," Chick said, holding his gaze steady on the words in front of him. "This is sad and beautiful. I like it. We need to build on it, but it's a nice foundation."

"I've got a melody I think we should use," Jadon said, springing up from the sofa and walking into the rehearsal room.

⌐≋⌐

"Meg, really . . . allow me," Devon said, taking the glass from Meg's hand.

Opening her refrigerator, Devon turned back toward Meg. "I see you have lemonade, many assorted colors of VitaminWater, and a nice looking red that really ought not be kept at this temperature," he said with a grin.

"Oh, how'd that get in there? Would you put it in the wine cooler? One of those orange VitaminWaters, please," Meg said, wiggling her finger to indicate it was nestled in the back behind the others.

"Orange it is. And because we are choosing by color, I will . . . choose . . . red," Devon said, pulling out the bottles before letting the door close on its own behind him.

Taking his time, he filled two glasses with ice and slowly poured their drinks. Walking into the living room, he placed the glasses on the table, and took a seat in the chair next to the sofa.

Silently letting out a breath of nervous energy, Meg sat on the sofa and tried not to let her eyes linger for too long on Devon. If he was the boogie man, the evil being everyone thought he was, he disguised it well.

Or was it that she just didn't want to see it? If she saw it, then she couldn't deny its presence.

Watching Devon rifle through his briefcase, Meg replayed the conversation she had with Flora that morning. It wasn't really a two-way conversation as much as it was a declaration by Flora, who then waited for Meg's very bewildered comments in return. As if their conversation had been recorded, Meg kept rewinding Flora's words. Every time she heard them, she winced. *"Meg. Today I woke up knowing that today this nightmare will end. Like a beast, it won't draw its last breath peacefully or passively. But it will end."*

"And what, may I ask, has you so off and in the clouds right now?" Devon asked, having been staring at Meg for some time without her even noticing.

Turning her head slowly in his direction, Meg hesitated in answering. "Ahh . . . just . . . nothing. More stuff that I can't understand. I'm sorry, were you saying something?"

Pressing his lips together in thought, Devon wrinkled his forehead and shook his head. "No, my dear, it was just an obvious observation that begged to be asked once I looked at you. So . . . back to the business at hand. Are you pleased?"

Meg tilted her head to one side. "Pleased?"

"Yes," Devon stretched out the word to emphasize how simple his question was.

"Yes, I am."

Devon smiled. "Very well. So it seems I *can* still do my job."

"And do it very well," Meg added. "As if there were ever any doubt in that."

Unable to hide his smile, Devon looked over his papers. "Where to start, where to start? You're all set for your photo shoot this afternoon at four o'clock? And did you receive the itinerary my assistant put together for you?"

"Yes and yes. Looks good."

"And Jadon will have no problems with how busy you will become?" Devon asked, giving Meg a gentle look of concern.

"No. He'll have no reason to be. He'll be with me," Meg said, pleased with Jadon's insistence on accompanying her during her revised book tour, and the band's unanimous decision to hold off on releasing their latest single until she and Jadon returned.

Devon forced his face to remain soft, "Oh, he will? That's even better."

Meg now kept her eyes fixed on Devon's face and his movements while he busied himself with more paper shuffling.

Stopping suddenly, Devon looked up at the wall in front of him, then at Meg, "Do you know Jadon's father very well?"

Startled by such a sharp change of subjects, Meg's head jerked slightly. "John? I've met him. He seems nice. A little scary at first . . ."

"Scary?"

Meg's head bobbed as she tried to think how best to describe the imposing figure that is John Hastings. "He's . . . well, he's nothing like Jadon, I can tell you that. Well, I take that back, maybe they are a bit alike. Emotionally, they seem to have some surprising similarities."

Sitting back into the chair, Devon crossed his legs and listened to Meg. He didn't know why the urge struck him so unexpectedly to ask about Jadon's father, but ever since listening to the message left on her answering machine, he couldn't let go of the nagging thought that Jadon's father was someone he needed to be careful of. So far, however, from what Meg was revealing, there was no reason for concern.

"So what is his occupation?" Devon asked.

"Oh, he is retired. He used to be a police detective. I like him. Even though he kind of takes your breath away when you first come face to face with him."

Tapping his finger against his mouth, Devon thought for a moment about Meg's last statement.

"I'm afraid I don't understand," he said.

"He's like a . . . walking, talking wall of a man. Physically speaking, he is the exact opposite of Jadon," Meg chuckled, taking another drink of her water.

Putting her glass back on the table, Meg looked up into Devon's silent stare. She curled her leg beneath her, sat up straighter on the sofa, and watched as his eyes tightened slightly. Meg could tell Devon was trying to visualize what she had just told him.

"Are you okay?" Meg asked.

"Wonderful. I'm wonderful. I was just . . . processing what you said. You created quite the image within my mind."

Meg laughed, "Oh . . . he is just as tall as you. I think he's a bit taller, in fact. But he's wide too. Scared the hell out of me when I first met him. Even though Jadon warned me. Where Jadon is so fair, John has dark skin and his eyes, hair and clothes are . . . black."

"And this John . . . Jadon's father . . . where does he live?" Devon asked, needing a moment to let the information settle into the deep recesses of his mind.

Although he was listening to Meg, Devon could feel the pieces of the puzzle fall painfully into place. It was brutally obvious Jadon's father had been tailing him, which meant he was suspicious of something. This meant if anything were to happen to Jadon, John Hastings would never take his scope off of Devon; instead, John would spend the rest of his life gunning for him. With the hum of Meg's voice washing over his thoughts while they raced quickly through his mind, Devon tried to expand his plan to embody the elimination of not one person, but two.

"Pardon me? What did you say, darling?" Devon asked abruptly, interrupting not only his own thoughts but Meg.

"I said he is coming back soon. I think later today. I think," Meg repeated. "Are you sure you are feeling all right? You really don't look well."

"Oh, nonsense. I'm perfectly fine. Although I have been tired lately. Could it be that we are actually feeling the effects of getting older?" Devon grinned, while biting down a million questions that begged to be voiced and answered. "I'm leaving town as soon as I leave here actually."

"Good. A little rest and relaxation."

"You could say that."

❧

Making her way off the dirt road and over the small, heavily wooded hill, Amanda dropped to her knees next to the tree where one week prior she had buried her weatherproof backpack under some fallen tree branches. Unzipping it quickly, she tried to ignore how cold she was. She hadn't anticipated it being such a cold day. But then, she questioned, does anyone visualize such a thing when they are thinking about killing someone?

Shaking her head, she tried to sweep away the thoughts that carried no value or meaning. Instead, she tried to focus in on the ones she had carefully rehearsed in her mind night after night. Pulling out the clothes she had meticulously packed, she looked down at her shirt and noticed the splattering of blood that dotted its surface.

As she fell back onto the ground, Amanda closed her eyes and let out a small, humorless laugh. She remembered the afternoon months ago when she walked into the small, dimly lit room to have her fortune told. She recalled the psychic telling her that soon she would carry out a well-rehearsed plan, a plan that would ultimately change the course of her life. Being the skeptic she was, Amanda asked what she would be wearing on that fateful day. Looking down at her shirt, she chuckled again.

"She said I would be wearing a light colored shirt, with dark red polka dots," Amanda whispered with a soft exhale.

As if watching the words take shape, then fade away into nonexistence, Amanda watched as her breath formed a translucent cloud, then dissipated into the cold autumn air.

"Shit. It's almost four o'clock. Have to go," Meg said, hitting *save* on her laptop, before she headed out the door for her photo shoot.

Walking into their house, Jadon looked around. Standing quietly in their living room, he wondered if it was just his imagination or if he really could still smell Devon. He knew the smell, even if he'd only caught its scent a handful of times. He hated the smell, even though he was very aware that most likely the cologne Devon wore was mind numbingly expensive he still found it repulsive.

According to Meg, her meeting with Devon went well. Nothing stood out as odd. Devon hadn't done or said anything that would be considered suspicious. Meg felt his motives were very clear, that he was there to help her with her book, plain and simple. Glancing around the room, Jadon wondered if he'd been wrong all along. *No. I'm not wrong,* he said to himself with a slow, resolute shake of his head.

Jadon tossed his pack of cigarettes and phone on the table, looked at the clock, and realized he'd have a couple hours before Meg would be done with her photo shoot. Wishing his dad were back already, Jadon decided to head over to his place for a while to work on the song some more. But more than anything, what he really wanted at the moment was to talk with his dad.

⌘

"Meg? Where are you honey?" Flora said quickly into the phone.

"I'm just stepping in for this photo shoot I have to do for that press conference coming up next month. Why? What's going on?"

"It's Erin. We're at the hospital. She's asking for you. It's the baby, Meg."

"I'll be right there. Tell her I'll be right there," Meg said with a sharp, frightened volume.

Standing motionless in the Media Imaging lobby, Meg felt her body ice over with panic.

"Ms. Scott . . . are you all right?" the receptionist asked.

Turning her head slowly, Meg felt her mind shut down with fear, making it hard to gather her thoughts. "I . . . no . . . my friend, she's been rushed to the hospital. I have to go. She's asking for me."

"Uh . . . oh boy, I think they're about ready to start," the receptionist said. "Just go . . . go . . . I'll tell them. Do you need someone to drive you?"

Meg shook her head, "No, thank you. No. I'm okay . . ."

With her body pushed forward by an unseen force, one that knew what it needed to do, Meg was oblivious to the heavy traffic that moved like snails between where she had just left and where she needed to go. Stepping out of her car in the hospital's parking lot, she was vaguely aware of the fact that she didn't remember finding a parking place, let alone one so close to the entrance. She slammed shut the car door, and with one forceful step swung her body in the direction of the hospital, and immediately fell hard onto the pavement. Puzzled, Meg looked up to see her purse strap caught in the car door. Wrestling to set it free, she tried to slow down her movements, her thoughts and the hands of time.

"Unlock the fucking door first. God, Meg. This is not a time to be a God damn moron," she cursed, attempting to talk herself through the process. Freeing her purse strap from the car, she turned and took heavy, determined steps across the parking lot. Once convinced her feet were steady, she broke into a full run.

Rounding the corner of the emergency room, Meg saw Flora and Chick standing outside of Erin's room. Keeping her focus cemented on Chick, Meg felt her body fall back into its instinctual rhythm of propelling her in the direction it needed to go. As she looked into his eyes, Meg felt the muscles in her face constrict.

"What happened?" She asked.

"She started to have these wicked contractions, out of nowhere. The doctor is in with her right now," Chick said, his voice cracking with worry.

"We just need to hear that Erin is stable. The baby will be okay, Chick. I know *he* will," Flora said.

Chick looked at Flora. Wrapping her arms around him, Flora knew she had said more than he was expecting to hear. Now instead of crying from fear alone, he also cried with joy.

"Let it out. She'll be okay," Flora said, "They both will be okay. The doctor is going to come out and say that. I know it."

Nodding his head, Chick wiped hard under his eyes. "You know that . . . and it's a boy?"

"It's a boy, honey," Flora said with an unquestioning nod.

Sliding her body down the wall and onto the floor, Meg cried with relief. Sliding his body next to hers, Chick let out a laugh through his tears.

Looking up at Flora, Meg asked, "You *know* this one, right? You *know*?"

"I *know*."

Hearing the door to Erin's room open, Chick and Meg scrambled to their feet and anxiously stood in front of the doctor while he walked out of her room and glanced once again at her chart.

"She'll be okay. We stopped her contractions. I really can't say why this happened. Her blood pressure had been good. We just saw her the other day. So it's a little bit more than puzzling. But, what's most important, is that she will be fine. And so is the baby. We're going to keep her overnight. Just for observation. You can go in and see her now," the doctor said, motioning toward the door.

Walking into the room, Flora, Meg and Chick looked at Erin and smiled at the sight of her lying peacefully on her bed.

"Hey . . . ," Chick said softly.

Opening her eyes, Erin wrinkled her forehead, then grinned at the sight of Chick's distraught face.

"I'm okay. So is little Chick," she said in a reassuring voice.

"Thank God. Thank you, God," Chick said, as his face lightly twisted again with tears.

"It's okay, baby. We're good. I don't know what triggered this. It came out of nowhere."

"Flora said you'd be okay. And the baby. She knew," Chick said, looking across Erin's bed at Flora. "She also . . . she knows the gender."

Erin looked up at Flora, "You do . . . ?"

"I'll let Chick share that bit of information. I'm going to leave you two. I need to make some calls. I have to let everyone know you're okay," Flora said, kissing Erin on the forehead.

Wiping the tears from her face, Meg sniffed before saying, "Yeah, I'm going to head back to the house. I want to tell Jadon. I'm going to grab some things, too. Because I'm coming back and spending as much time as I can with you before they kick me out. So, I'll be back. I love you Erin . . . I was so scared." She stopped to choke back her tears, "I was terrified. I couldn't get to you fast enough. I'll be back though. I'll be back."

Meg closed the door quietly behind her, walked down the hall, and took another deep sigh of relief. Nodding at the nurses gathered behind the counter, she didn't hear her name being called repeatedly. When she finally realized that someone was trying to get her attention, she stopped quickly. Turning around, Meg watched as Dr. Solomon waved his hand at her and walked quickly in her direction.

"I'm so happy to see you, Meg. Do you have a minute?" Dr. Solomon asked.

"Uh, yeah. Sure. Is it Erin?" Meg said, confused.

"No, Meg. It's you. We received your blood work from your last checkup. Everything looks perfect, Meg. Everything. However, something has happened that I hadn't quite thought possible due to some of the damage you incurred. But . . . it happened and I'm going to need to set you up with a specialist who will be handling it."

"Oh. Well this doesn't sound so good." Meg said, feeling a bit unsteady.

"You're pregnant, Meg."

Chapter 22

Ending the call, John slid his phone back in his pocket and scanned the busy storefronts of downtown Bay City. He replayed in his mind all the pieces of information his old friend on the force had just told him, all the while blindly glancing at each of the many faces hurrying down the sidewalk. Taking a long measured breath, he silently thanked God. Not only was he right in believing that Devon was the master puppeteer pulling the strings attached to George Strum, but now he had the evidence to support it. Strum's attorney, Blake Wilson, is on the board of Langley Communication. One of the largest shareholders at Langley Communication is Devon Hathaway. And to make things even more interesting, his source discovered that Wilson, although still licensed, no longer practiced law. Unless, of course, an old prep school pal calls him up and calls in a favor.

No one knows what moves people to do certain things, but John was very grateful his friend felt so moved as to scour over every minute detail having to do with George Strum, even delving into the obvious matter of how Strum's significant legal fees were being paid. And, his friend learned, it was not the impoverished George Strum who was paying Wilson's exorbitant fees. There were no bank accounts in Strum's name, domestic or foreign, making payments to Wilson. Yet, Wilson's bill was always kept current, paid from by wire transfer from oversees. Although his friend had yet to connect Devon to these payments, the one thing he knew was that they weren't coming from Strum.

But the deepest nail driven into Devons' coffin came unwittingly from Wilson's own receptionist. As it happened, Wilson's receptionist was unfamiliar with the resourcefulness of a detective trying to get information without a search warrant. But, she was all too familiar with the drudgery of doing her boss's weekly time sheet. Making certain every minute was billed to the correct client was a daunting task. So it made sense when one of the women detectives at the station posed as Devon's assistant and innocently asked for help in making sense of Mr. Hathaway's phone log. Wilson's assistant, as a professional courtesy and offering all the assistance she could, faxed over her boss's complete phone log for the last month. And the phone records showed that Devon was receiving calls from Wilson daily.

John asked that the phone log be faxed to Meg's house; he wanted to show it to Meg personally. And he wanted her to have it in hand when confronting Devon — although, he wasn't about to let her confront him alone. Turning on to Mandalay Bay Drive, John was relieved to see Jadon's Porsche sitting in his driveway.

Pulling his truck behind Jadon's car, John cut the engine and exhaled deeply. He was given the answers he'd asked for, leaving him to safely conclude that there was a God after all: one that listens and speaks. Now all he had to do was get those answers into the hands of those who needed them the most. And by doing so, honoring Emily's request - looking after their son.

Hitting his head hard against the steering wheel, John tried to make sense of the immeasurable pain that burned through his slumped chest. His skin tingled in shock as his body steadily grew heavier. He moved his hand across his chest. Staring at his blood covered hand; he lifted his head slightly trying to make sense of what just happened. As his vision grew narrow within the graying veil of unconsciousness, he watched Devon walk toward Jadon's front door.

Without the hint of noise, Devon closed the door behind him, and moved silently into Jadon's house. Standing at the end of the hallway that opened into the expansive living room, he stared at his target and took a peaceful deliberate moment to record Jadon's movements while he sat behind the piano facing the ocean. Realizing he couldn't afford to waste time, he moved his body slowly closer, lifting his arms, he took aim.

Jumping to the sound of Big Larry's dramatic bark, Jadon stopped his hands on the keyboard, wondering why Meg had returned early.

"Oh good Meg. You're back," Jadon said, looking out over the ocean.

"That I am," Devon replied.

Startled by the voice, Jadon knew this was not a friendly visit. Instead it was the culmination of his fears. Devon was making his appearance to settle things, for good. Devon knew Meg would be gone; he was the one who set up her photo shoot. Jadon spun slowly around until he was able to meet eyes with Devon.

"Ah, a gun. I suppose you have plans for that," Jadon said, motioning with his eyes at the pistol held steady in his direction.

"Yes, I have very specific plans. Thank you for the inquiry."

"Good to know I wasn't going crazy. I knew you weren't helping Meg because you were this *great guy*," Jadon chuckled. "So what's your big diabolical plan, Dev? Kill me, then drag me off? Or leave my dead body for Meg to find later? Then of course you're all ready to console her. Is that how your plan goes . . . ?"

"Something like that. But unlike the crime shows you Americans busy yourself with on the telly, I'm not about to stand here and divulge the intricate workings of how this will play out. I find all that unnecessary dialogue nauseating. Besides, the only one within range of my voice is you, and, well . . . I really don't care what you think. You've caused far too much trouble already. You and your father, that is," Devon said in a drawn out hiss.

"My father? Where is he?" Jadon's voice rose.

"He's fine. He's . . . resting."

~

Biting hard at the loose skin on her bottom lip, Meg recalled repeatedly the words Dr. Solomon had just told her. *You're pregnant, Meg.* The sounds of the words created myriad images that filled her mind; each image filled her heart with excited joy causing her chest to tremble and a laugh to escape from the grin resting on her face.

"Mom . . . did you hear that? Did you . . . Oh, my God. I'm so happy. As long as I can carry this baby full term. But . . . it's a miracle that I'm even pregnant. God doesn't give you a miracle, then suddenly take it away, does she?" Meg questioned in whispered words not meant to be heard by anyone. "Jadon . . . He's going to be . . . Oh, God. Thank you. Thank you."

Swinging her car into the driveway outside her house, she stared through the trees, and tried to make out whose vehicle was parked in Jadon's driveway. Walking across her lawn, she smiled when she recognized that it was John's truck. Leaning her body around one of the tall bushes bordering Jadon's driveway, Meg tried to look inside the truck.

Smiling when she saw Lil' Larry turn and look in her direction, her smile quickly faded once her eyes focused on Jadon's father, slumped against his steering wheel.

"Oh, my God. Oh, my God," Meg said in a frantic whisper.

Rushing to the driver's side of the truck, Meg flung open the door, and tried to make sense of the horrific image sitting before her. Her body trembling in fear, she ran her hand over John's arm.

"Please don't be dead. Please don't be dead. Please don't be dead. Why aren't you moving? Why aren't you moving?" Meg repeated in a voice fueled by panic.

Forcing her body to move, Meg struggled to shake John into consciousness. Producing no movement, she slowly removed her hand from his body. Looking down in terror she saw the blood covering her fingers and palm.

"911, 911. I have to call 911," Meg's mouth trembled.

Looking for help, Meg saw John's cell phone nestled inside his front shirt pocket. Quickly she punched the numbers needed to get help

"I need help. I need help. Someone's been shot. Mandalay Bay Drive," Meg shrieked hoarsely. "No, I don't know if they're alive or not. I can't tell . . . I can't . . . I don't know . . ." She paused to listen to the 911 dispatcher. "I'm trying to feel for a pulse, but my hand is trembling, I can't tell. Oh, God. Oh, God. Help me! Oh, God!"

Hearing Meg's strained scream for help, John slowly opened his eyes.

"Meg," he whispered in a shallow voice.

"He's alive!" Meg screamed. "He said my name."

"Meg. You . . . need . . . to take . . . my gun, Meg. My gun. It's Devon, Meg. He's going to kill Jadon," John struggled to say.

Dropping the phone, Meg stood motionless. John's words struck her chest like a bullet. Unable to breathe, she stood frozen in place.

"Meg. Tell . . . Jadon." John paused to find the strength to continue. "Tell him . . . I love him."

Meg watched as John closed his eyes, and his body dropped heavier against the steering wheel. Running to the passenger side of the truck, Meg threw open the door and saw the large pistol sitting next to Lil Larry. Reaching across the seat, she grabbed the heavy revolver and held it in her hands.

Running up the stairs leading into Jadon's house, Meg opened the door; her movements changing from clumsy with panic, to smooth and fluid. Her thoughts shifted with intensity onto what she needed to do.

Meg slipped into the house and moved quietly through the entryway toward the living room. Keeping herself hidden behind the hallway wall, Meg felt her eyes well up with tears of rage as she listened to the venomous words flowing from Devon.

Glancing through the opening between the living room and kitchen, Meg could make out the shadowy images reflected on the windows overlooking the beach. With his gun poised and ready, Devon stood with his arms held with a steady aim at Jadon, who was sitting at his piano. Looking down at the large revolver, Meg wrapped both hands firmly around the grip, and held it tight to her chest while trying to harness her rapid breath. Swallowing hard, she straightened her stance, and walked out from the hallway. In one liquid motion, she lifted the gun, and extended both arms in a marked stance, locking on to her target as she walked swiftly behind Devon.

Holding her aim, she said in a low, weathered voice, "Turn around."

"Meg," Jadon said in shock.

Keeping his eyes, and gun leveled on Jadon, Devon tried to hide the wave of surprise he felt by Meg's magical appearance. "Darling. I don't know what you're planning on doing, but . . . I think you might want to think long and hard before you do something we both know you'll regret."

"Turn around," she repeated.

"Meg, where did you get that? Meg, just walk away. Please. I'm begging you," Jadon whispered, pleading with his words and eyes.

Glancing at his gentle face, Meg felt an inner force well inside her, causing her back to stiffen, preparing itself for the recoil the gun was about to make.

"We both know you won't be able to live with yourself if you shoot me or anyone else for that matter. It's just simply not who you are," Devon said softly, but with an air of annoyance.

"Turn the fuck around."

Conceding, but only partially, Devon stepped to the side, keeping his gun held steady on Jadon, but his eyes fixed on Meg. Tilting his head to show he had obliged and honored her peculiar request; Devon cast a quick glance at Jadon, then back at her.

Meg felt time suspend itself; no longer could she hear the emphatic words streaming from Jadon, but in an odd shift of reality, she could hear the clock ticking loudly and slowly in Jadon's kitchen. Allowing herself only a moment to look into Devon eyes, Meg dropped her gaze back onto his chest.

"Meg . . . Be careful with that," Devon said, hearing the solid, heavy click when Meg pulled back on the hammer and cocked the gun. "I love you. You know that. And we both know you'll never be able to live with yourself if you kill me."

"I'll never be able to live with myself if I don't," she said.

With the release of an explosive bullet, Devon's body hit the wall hard behind him. As his body dropped to the floor Meg dropped the gun.

Rushing to Meg, Jadon grabbed her hands and held them tightly within his own. Feeling the heat left on her skin by the gun, he looked at her palms.

"Meg. My God, there's blood on your hand. What . . . what the hell, how did that get there? Christ," Jadon said, his trembling voice mimicking his hands as they shook trying to cradle hers

"Your dad," Meg cried. "He's . . . been shot. Devon shot him. John told me to use his gun. He said to tell you . . . *that he loved you*." Falling to her knees, she held her head in her hands while the emotional impact of the last few moments crashed against her body.

"Wha . . . What…. Where is he? What . . . ?" Jadon said in a confused stupor, falling onto his knees in front of Meg. "Jesus Christ. I got to . . . I got go to him."

Taking Meg's hands, Jadon pulled them both up and out the door. As the sirens in the distance drew closer, Jason reached inside the truck and held his dad in his arms.

Chasing Nirvana

Chapter 23

Meg ran behind Jadon through the opened doors of the emergency room, trying to keep up with his rapid strides. Throwing his weight against the counter at the nurse's station, Jadon asked in a breathless voice where they'd taken his father. As if in a fog, Meg noticed the nurse's arm move, and motion down the hall. Taking Jadon's hand, she watched as he turned to look at her before rushing them both down the long corridor leading to where John was.

Letting go of Jadon, Meg ran her fingers through her hair, and noticed her right hand was trembling uncontrollably. She lifted her head and watched as Jadon tried to get answers from the nurses and technicians leaving and entering the white curtain surrounding his dad. Turning her heavy head slowly to the right then back to the left, Meg watched as the walls struggled to keep their solid shape. Squinting, she tried to make out the words yelled by the doctors. She couldn't make sense of any of them, but she could still hear the clock clicking loudly and slowly from inside Jadon's kitchen.

"Meg?" Chick said in disbelief, as he held a small bag of Erin's belongings in his hand. "What the fuck is going on . . . who is that . . . what's . . ."

Taking a forced swallow, Meg tried to dampen her paper dry mouth. "That's . . . John," she said putting her hand on the wall to steady her.

Wrapping his arm around her, Chick held her tight, while absorbing the dire situation. "Fuck. What the fuck? Where's Jay?"

Looking around, Chick located a chair, unused and out of place in the hallway. Moving Meg slowly, he eased her body onto the chair and looked at her hands, then back into her eyes.

"Devon's gone," she said.

Staring at her, Chick repeated quietly what Meg had said. Looking back down at her hand, Chick ran his fingers across the dried blood stained on her palm.

"That's . . . that's not his. That's not Devon's," Meg whispered.

Turning to look over his right shoulder, Chick watched as Jadon walked swiftly toward them, then dropped onto his knees in front of Meg. Resting his head on her leg, he cried. Feeling her face tighten, Meg tried to hold back the tears. Too forceful to contain, they emerged in uncontrollable surges. Jadon looked up at her and ran his hand down her cheek, gently pulling her hair away from her face. Lifting her right hand he kissed her palm.

Meg struggled to say something, anything, that would ease his pain. Shaking his head, he held her fingers at his mouth and said, "He's going to make it. He's . . . going to make it. They said if it had been a minute longer, he'd be gone. But . . . he's going to make it."

Catching her breath, Meg felt her body strengthen. "They said that? He's . . ."

Jadon nodded. "He's unconscious, but they have a heartbeat. The bullet missed his heart. I held his hand, Meg. I felt it tighten on mine."

The sound of running steps approached them. It was Flora, moving quickly in Meg's direction. Seeing the chaos and people gathered, she felt her heart tighten.

"Meg!" Flora said in a softened scream. "Meg."

"Someone tell me what the hell is going on," Chick said, running his hand through his hair as he stepped aside to make room for Flora.

"It's over. It's over," Flora whispered in a lull as she rocked Meg softly in her arms.

⤳

Meg shifted in her seat in the hospital waiting room, as she waited outside the emergency room where Jadon was sitting with his father. Turning her right hand palm side up, she examined its surface. Curling her fingers inward, she made a fist then released it. Rubbing her left hand across her right arm, she felt the weak muscles tremble from strain.

Her fixed inspection of her hand was broken when Flora took the seat next to her and handed Meg a steaming paper cup with a tea bag floating inside.

"I know you like coffee. But I figured your nerves have already been put through hell today. Are the detectives done speaking with you?" Flora asked.

Meg nodded, while wrapping her hands around the hot cup of water.

Looking down at her own cup of tea, then turning her gaze so that it fell mindlessly across the room full of visitors, Flora released a long drawn out breath. "You did what you needed to do."

"I know," Meg said, still not lifting her eyes.

Turning to look directly at Meg, Flora ran her hand over Meg's arm. "You took your life back."

Meg chuckled through her tears. "Yeah."

"Meg . . . don't be worried."

"I know what I did was right. God . . . he was going to . . . kill Jadon," Meg struggled with the words.

"No sweetheart, not that. I meant don't be worried about the baby."

Meg lifted her head quickly, turned in her chair and faced Flora. "You know . . . "

"I know . . . I'm right, I take it," Flora smiled.

"Yes. I just found out. Dr. Solomon told me as I was leaving Erin earlier."

Meg caught her breath as the wave of tears rolled over her body. Starting to weep, she whispered vulnerably, "What . . . what do you see? Do you see anything?"

Flora nodded with a smile.

Holding her hand over her mouth, Meg couldn't stop the emotion tumbling through her voice, "Do I . . . carry it full . . ."

"I'm going to tell you what I see. It's a very clear image. It sits with clear, crisp lines within my mind. Close your eyes . . . I want you to see it too."

Staring first into Flora's gentle eyes, Meg then closed her own and held tightly onto Flora's hands.

Taking her time, Flora closed her eyes and brought back the vision that had been appearing to her repeatedly over the last two weeks.

"This is what I see Meg. I see long brown hair flowing freely behind the silhouette of a beautiful little girl." Pausing for a moment, Flora felt her own emotion stifle her words. "She is walking hand in hand with her parents. They are walking along the beach. But they don't live near the water. This is a trip. They are on a trip. And she is excited. She is laughing. More than her beauty and gentle, delicate frame, I see her energy - it rivals that of her mother and her mother's mother. She will be a fighter."

Flora chuckled lightly. "She will spin her father around in circles many, many times. Oh . . . I like her name. It feels good. Don't ask, dear, I won't be telling it to you. She is the embodiment of a great deal of love. And not just from her parents. I see the love of many people circling around her. She is gifted Meg. Oh . . . the three of you are happy."

Flora stopped, her hands tightened on Meg's. Opening her eyes slightly, Meg made sure Flora was still resting in her peaceful, meditative state and safely closed her own eyes and waited.

Humming first, Flora smiled and began to rock gently back and forth as if listening to a song that only she heard. "Ch . . . Ch . . . Ch . . . ," she said in a soft, velvet tone that only Meg could hear.

Meg opened her eyes to the familiar sound, then quickly closed them again, not wanting to disrupt the flow of energy moving through Flora.

"I know. Here I am again. Oh, sweetness, my dear baby girl . . . I am so very proud of you. You took back your life. You have given us both wings to fly," Flora said in conclusion.

⤛

"My dad's holding steady, Erin is sleeping like a baby . . . and I don't want to go anywhere near our two houses," Jadon said with an exhausted smile, as he tapped at the steering wheel cradled in front of him.

Meg chuckled. "I don't either."

"Chick said we could stay at their place. He'd probably like the company. I'm sure he's antsy without Erin. Even though he's busy chasing the two Larrys around. But . . . I just don't want . . ."

"Me neither. Let's go somewhere new. Some place away from the forceful winds of the ocean. Some place far away from what just happened. The images of what happened earlier are still flashing in my mind. I don't want to focus on them, not right now. It's like trying to stare at the sun: the images are still too bright. I just want to let them fade a bit. If they can. Part of me wants to be where it all started, all the good . . . I mean. I love the memories we've made there. But . . . the memories from today . . . they will always be standing to the side of the old, beautiful ones."

With the smile of an excited boy about to embark on a new adventure, Jadon turned to look at Meg, "Maybe we can find a place . . . up in the mountains. Maybe not as remote as my dad's place, but . . . like Flora and Raffi's. Something nestled in between the trees. I like that idea. Kind of like nature is holding us in its hand."

Not knowing when the perfect moment would arrive, Meg felt her body swirl with excitement as she turned to face Jadon.

"I like that idea. I like it more than you know," she said, her eyes welling with tears.

"It's okay. It's okay." Leaning toward her, Jadon wrapped his arms tightly around her tired body and whispered into her ear. "It's okay. This day is going to take a lot of time to overcome. If it happened in a movie, I'd hardly have believed it. Yet, it happened to us - in one day."

Lightly shaking her head no, Meg knew the thoughts resting on her heart weren't the ones he was thinking. "Remember when I said, I thought you'd be a wonderful father," she whispered softly.

"Yeah," Jadon said, pulling his head back lightly to look delicately into her eyes. "I remember. But that's okay. As long as I have you, I'm good."

"All my life . . . ," Meg kept her tone soft and deliberate, "I've pictured heaven. But it's been . . . out there," she said, fluttering her hand lightly in front of her. "At times I would give paradise to the characters in my novels, I'd let them taste heaven. Sometimes I would be so sad, so sad that I didn't get to have it for myself, that I would write a story where they, too, were denied a happy ending." Putting her hand on her chest, Meg caught her breath and continued. "It's like

I've been chasing something. I never knew what really. But I've been running, and trying to catch up with it. Nirvana. I've been chasing after my own nirvana. And now . . . sitting here, right now, in this very moment . . . I've caught up with it."

Rubbing his hand along her face, Jadon smiled and kissed her tears. "Me, too. I have you, and because of you Meg . . . I have my dad. I can't even begin to tell you what that means to me. I don't think it's fully sunken in yet. I have so much to say to him." He paused to kiss her lips, then her closed eyelids, before trying to look into her eyes again. "But now, I have both you and my father. And I am so thankful to God, Fate . . . whatever the hell it's called."

Soaking up the world that lives within his eyes, Meg breathed in Jadon's words before voicing her own, "There's something else to be thankful for . . ."

The End